FALSE FLAG

One Hundred Years of Deception

A NOVEL

JAY BARRETT

HALLARD PRESS

Editing: Hallard Press LLC/Paula F. Howard
Cover Design by Hallard Press LLC/John W Prince

Page Design, Typography & Production by Hallard Press LLC/John W Prince

Published by Hallard Press LLC.
www.HallardPress.com   Info@HallardPress.com   352-775-1143

Bulk copies of this book can be ordered by contacting Hallard Press LLC,
Info@HallardPress.com

Printed in the United States of America   .

ISBN: 978-1-951188-05-4

JAY BARRETT

For Barbara Jane
1932 - 2018

A loving wife for 63 years.

False Flag (used together) meaning. 1.a covert operation designed to deceive; the deception creates the appearance of a particular party, group, or nation being responsible for some activity, disguising the actual source of responsibility.

Prologue

The waters were dark and placid that night in the year 1898. On Sunday, February 15th, in Havana Harbor at 21:39 hours, the only sound and light came from whining generators and a dim glow of newly installed carbon filament bulbs aboard the *USS Maine.* Anchored offshore in untroubled waters, the 6,789-ton 2nd class battleship floated quietly. The moon was hidden.

One moment later, at 21:40 hours, a double explosion ripped her apart sending her to the bottom, along with 260 of her 355-man crew. Only 16 sailors escaped uninjured.

The following month a Naval Court of Inquiry declared she was destroyed by a Spanish naval mine despite Spain's claim that the sinking was a U.S. False Flag. On April 25, 1898, Congress voted to go to war with Spain.

Seventy-six years later, in 1974, motivated by the False Flag war with Vietnam, Admiral Hyman Rickover opened a new investigation into the sinking of the *Maine.* The National Security Agency, while pretending to cooperate, secretly sought to find and destroy an item that would expose the truth about what happened that night so long ago: a diary written onboard the *Maine* on the day it was destroyed.

Chapter 1

I was relaxed, driving my new black Mustang Mach 1 south on Route 93 from Warren, New Hampshire, to Boston's North End. Cruising down a tree-lined, snow-banked, four-lane highway, I could never reach the darkness beyond my headlights. It was March 12, 1972. The time was 10:55 p.m. Little did I know that two hours later I would receive a phone call to put me on an even darker road with the National Security Agency.

Ellen, my live-in girlfriend, reclined in the passenger seat, napping with the front of her slouchy white knit ski cap pulled over her eyes. At least I thought she was napping. After skiing all day, it was a reasonable thing to assume. But when I stopped at the end of the North End off ramp, Ellen sat up, pushed her cap off her eyes, and faced me. Her clear, unblinking eyes didn't look like someone who had just woken up.

"Tony, we've been going together for almost two years,"

"Yes, we have, Beautiful."

"Well, where's this relationship going?"

"I think it's going pretty good."

"Take me to my mother's house."

"You want to go to your mother's?"

"You heard me."

"Okay. Okay."

When we arrived at her mother's house, she got out of the car as I reached for my door to help. "Stay in the car. I don't need your help."

What she really meant was: "I don't need you."

Ellen reached into the back seat, yanked out her ski boots and overnight bag, then slammed the door. She put everything on the porch and came back, took her skis and poles off the roof of the car, then took everything into the house. There was no "goodnight" or goodnight kiss. Ellen was pissed, and I was tired. When the door to the house closed and kitchen light came on, I knew she was safely inside.

"Good night, Beautiful ," I whispered.

My off-street parking space was two blocks from my flat. I took my overnight bag out and locked my skis in the car. It was midnight with no moon; the darkness was broken by light from a streetlamp a half block from my front steps. Surrounded by cold, gloomy brick buildings on both sides of the street, I walked to my building. The only thing that moved, was fine-grained snow skimming along the ground in the lead.

Maybe a bit paranoid at the midnight hour, I removed my ski glove, took my Glock 17 out the ski bag, and kept my hand on it as I slipped it into my ski jacket pocket. You can't pick the time or place to become a target when someone you helped get free room and board for life wants revenge. Anyway, I made it home safely.

But two months ago , it was a different story, the walk from my car to my flat wasn't so pleasant. On that night, an escaped lifer, I should have recognized, popped out of the alley that ran along the far side of my building, and although not everyone who comes out of an alley at night is a bad guy, something just didn't feel right. I was across the street, alongside a brick building forty yards away. He turned and faced me. I had taken my Glock out of my jacket pocket and held it where he couldn't see it. So, when he raised his right arm, I catapulted into the brick wall as a bullet buzzed my ear, spitting brick chips into the side of my face. He never got to take aim again. I dropped him with a bullet to his heart. No more bad prison meals for him.

Ahh, memories. I unlocked my front door and entered. When Ellen and I left three days ago, I had turned down the heat. Now, the temperature inside was suitable for a polar bear. I turned the heat back up, changed into a long-sleeved tee shirt and sweatpants, crawled under two blankets and fell asleep.

When the phone rang, I figured it was less than an hour since I left Ellen and it was probably her calling, so I let it ring. But after five rings, I groaned and picked up. "Yeah. "

"Mr. April?" asked a voice I didn't know.

"Yes?"

"I sincerely apologize for calling you at this late hour, but it is very urgent that I meet with you tonight."

I was intrigued by her educated, intelligent, high-class Katharine Hepburn voice.

"Mr. April, are you there?"

"Yes. Did you say tonight?"

"Yes. My chauffeur, Henry, is parked outside your home. He can bring you here to Weston, and back to your home, all within two hours."

"Ma'am, it's freezing out, and it's one in the morning. Can't we meet later in the day?"

"I am leaving in four hours. Colonel Wilson recommended that I call you. He led me to believe you would go anywhere at any time."

Chuck Wilson and I were in Army Special Forces (airborne) together. We met when the 8th Special Forces Group was formed as a Latin American counter insurgency group at Fort Gulick in the Panama Canal Zone.

"I haven't seen or heard from Chuck in years, and I've mellowed."

At the mention of Chuck's name, I had already made up my mind to go, but wanted to see how urgent it was for her to see me.

"Mr. April, would a $5,000 retainer get you out in the cold?"

"Yes, it would. What is it you want?"

"I prefer not to talk over the phone."

Obviously, this woman was used to getting her way. "Let me check to see if your man has arrived."

I shivered over to the kitchen window on a cold wooden oak floor and peaked out from behind the shade. A windswept, fine-grained snow was still blowing down the street. A limo was parked under a streetlamp half a block from my front door. I could see the engine was running from exhaust vapor dancing in the wind.

"There's a black Bentley outside."

"Yes, that's my automobile."

"Ok, I'll be down in fifteen minutes. I need to shower and have a cup of coffee."

"I will inform Henry. There is some information on the back seat for you to read. It will help you understand why I need your services. I look forward to meeting you, Mr. April."

"Who am I meeting with? Hello? Hello!"

Damn, she'd hung up. In 1974, there was no caller ID, so I couldn't call her back. I looked out the window; the Bentley was still there. While Mr. Coffee fired up, I took a hot shower. Then, gulped down a cup of black coffee as I dressed.

In fifteen minutes, I was out the door, just stopping briefly at the outer doorway to contemplate my sanity. The area sheltered me from the wind but not the bitter cold. Then, pulling up my topcoat collar and jerking down the hat brim over my forehead, I stepped out. Head down, I turned toward where the limo was parked, and after a few steps, expected Henry to pull up. Figuring he had to have seen me since I was the only nut out in the city at this hour. I looked up. There was no limo; nothing under the streetlamp but a circle of light.

I stopped, looked down, then up the abandoned street again. Nothing. No one. No sense standing in a cold, windy street trying to figure out what was going on. I dashed back to my doorway and hung for a couple of minutes. If it hadn't been for the mention of Chuck Wilson, I wouldn't have stayed even that long. One more look up and down the deserted street, then I went in and back to bed.

Chapter 2

Iawoke two hours later than usual at 8:30 a.m. The light, brightening off-white plaster walls of my bedroom, announced the coming of another day. The ancient steam radiator of this century-old red brick building hissed loudly, slaving to push the room temperature above sixty. Weak sunlight, contributing no heat, slid through the gaps of lowered shades covering windows that faced Boston Harbor. Half asleep, I reached over to Ellen's side of the bed, then remembered why she wasn't with me, and sighed.

Rolling onto my back, I stared up at the aging plaster ceiling and replayed Katharine Hepburn's call in my head:

A woman, I'm sure I never met, calls at one a.m. saying it's urgent to see me. Doesn't say why. Makes her connection to me through Chuck Wilson. Where has Chuck been in these last five years? I haven't even talked to him since leaving Panama. How Chuck operates, though, he would know what I do, and where.

She sends Henry, her chauffeur, to take me to Weston. He gets here in a black Bentley. In the time it takes me to get down to the street from my apartment, Henry and the Bentley disappear. Did she call Henry off? If she did, something must have happened in the twelve minutes between the end of her call and my getting down to the street. She doesn't call again, so she's not surprised that I don't show. Yet she insisted that I meet with her last night. What happened to the urgency? I can't call her because she hung up on me before I could get her name or phone number. I decide Bob will help me find her.

I have a racquetball match at 11:00 a.m. with chunky Bob Berry, a Boston police detective. We grew up together and are best friends. For an Irish kid and an Italian kid to be friends in the 1940's was unusual.

After graduating high school, Bob joined the Boston Police Department. I went on to Northeastern University School of Law, Co-op and ROTC programs. My year of Co-op was with the Criminal Division of the United States Justice Department, but I wasn't interested in becoming a lawyer. My goal was to become a Private Investigator.

When I graduated, I served my obligatory three years in the military. After a tour in Vietnam, I was accepted by the Army Special Forces (Airborne) at Fort Bragg, North Carolina. Upon graduation, I was assigned to Fort Gulick in the Panama Canal Zone where I met Colonel Chuck Wilson. Our mission was training the Latin Americans in counter-insurgency warfare. Most of my tour was spent in the mountains and jungles of Ecuador.

The day I left the service, Bob had met me at the airport. I still remembered the conversation:

"Good to have you home, Tony."

"Thanks. You're looking happy and healthy. Sandra and the kids good?"

"Sandra is good. The kids are growing like weeds. They can hardly wait to see their Uncle Tony. I expected you'd be coming home married to Bonita."

"Came close. Have you seen my mother lately?"

"Yesterday. I didn't say anything about you coming home."

"How is she?"

"Honestly? Not good. Her conversation with me was more detached than ever. There's no room in her mind for anything other than Michael and Maria."

Michael, my father, was killed serving in the Army Air Force during World War II. He was 24 years old, and mother was pregnant with Maria. Five-years after he was killed, Maria was taken from a neighborhood playground, molested and murdered. At the time she was abducted, my mother, Laura, was helping bandage another girl's knee and had left Maria unattended for less than a minute. She never forgave herself. On the day they found Maria dead, I knelt down and swore to God that I would find Maria's killer.

"Bob, I can't say I'm surprised. When I called her and said I was coming home to stay, she didn't react at all, just rattled on about a children's book she was reading."

"Now that you're out of the service, what are you going to do?"

"I'm sure I can get back into Justice. In two years, I'll have my PI license. Then I'm going after that no-good bastard who molested and killed Maria."

"Tony, I have done everything I was allowed to do, and more, to find that scum. In the Special Forces, you were tracking and confronting men that slithered through the jungle like poisonous snakes. Look out the window, Tony. You may not see it, but it's a jungle out there, too. I work every day tracking down and confronting dirt bags."

"So, what are you telling me?"

"I am telling you, that when you get your Private Investigator license, we'll partner up. Now, I have to walk the fine line of department regulations, but you won't have to. Together, we can take more dirt bags off the streets, and have a better shot at finding Maria's killer."

Two years later, Maria's killer was arrested and convicted, and while gratifying, it had turned brutal. Bob had arrested a pedophile, and while searching the perp's house found a naked picture of Maria. Whoever had taken the picture had attempted to make her smile. Her tear-streaked face revealed a frightened little five-year-old girl with a forced closed-lips smile. Seeing it made my mouth foam like a rabid dog. Bob determined the pedophile was not the one who had taken the picture, and the scumbag couldn't remember who had given him the photo. It had been my job to refresh his memory.

On the night the pedophile made bail, and was released, I knocked on his third-floor tenement door. He opened the door wide with a smile like he was expecting company. I observed a clean kitchen with a red and grey linoleum covered floor, four metal red vinyl cushioned chairs set around a red metal expandable table, and a white four-burner range. On the table were two glasses, a bottle of white wine, three lighted pillar candles, and a vase with a single yellow rose.

The bald, baby-faced, half-pint suddenly realized by my squinted eyes and tight lips that I wasn't a friendly visitor, and tried to close the door. I pushed my way through, grabbed him by the throat, and shoved the featherweight across the room over to the kitchen stove.

"Who gave you the picture?" I demanded, pushing his head down sideways on an unlit burner. I shoved Maria's picture in his twisted face. He just groaned.

"Ok, asshole, you want to go up in flames, it's all right by me." I put the picture in my pocket and reached over his head to turn on the gas.

"Stop! I'll tell you! I'll tell you!"

He dropped a dime on a bespeckled, bald, ugly forty-three-year-old college economics professor. Bob's search of the professor's apartment uncovered more pictures of Maria and two other young girls he had also molested and murdered.

Later, the professor was sentenced to life in prison, but I wanted him dead. Bob kept me away from the fuck. He knew prisoners wouldn't let a child molester and killer, live for long. Within three months, the pedophile was dead, stabbed to death in the shower.

Sadly, the trial's graphic evidence and testimony proved too much for my mother. She died shortly afterwards from a cerebral embolism at the age of fifty-two.

Now, a while since she passed, I was on my way to play racquetball with Bob, anxious to talk about my early morning Weston phone call. It was a cold, crisp, sunny day. Temperatures were in the high twenties. The wind had died down to a whisper. Snow dust had gathered in doorways and corners of buildings. With daylight, the street was filled with people and parked cars. The North End was awake as I bumped through it.

At one end of my street there's a small grocery store. The owner, Mr. Martinelli, was standing outside in the freezing weather with no hat, no coat, just a long-sleeved white dress shirt tucked into baggy pants. He had to be seventy years old or better, but his lean six-foot body didn't even shiver.

Mr. Martinelli liked to observe what was going on in the neighborhood. When a stranger came into the neighborhood, he always knew whether they were a tourist, a businessperson, or someone up to no good. He had alerted me several times before about trouble hanging around my apartment building.

"*Buongiorno,* Signor Martinelli."

"*Buongiorno,* Anthony ."

He's known me since I was a little kid, and we share the same first name, Anthony, my proper given name. Also, my father, Michael, worked part-time for Mr. Martinelli while attending Northeastern University. He loved my father. It had brought us close.

Every time we meet, he asks to see the photograph of my father that I carry in my wallet.

"Anthony, show me the picture."

The photo shows my father standing with his crew below the nose of their B-26 Marauder. Above them, "Laura's Guys" was painted in two-foot high letters. During the war, there wasn't a week that went by without my mother sending Dad and all the crew a care package. They became known as "Laura's Guys". In the photo, he was wearing his Army Air Corp uniform, Captain bars on his shoulders, silver wings and ribbons pinned to the chest of his jacket. I don't know when the picture was taken, but I do know that on May 12, 1944, he flew out of Corsica and was shot down over Fondi, Italy. The airplane exploded and no one survived. He died just seven days after his twenty-fourth birthday. I was four years old, and my sister Maria, was just born. He never got to hold his little Maria.

In his letters home, father told of how he kept us close to him on every mission. He would put his wallet, with our picture, in the breast pocket of his flight suit. When I was twelve years old, I got a wallet for Christmas. Ever since, I have carried two photos with me—a copy of the yellowing, black and white picture of mom, dad, and me that he carried on the day he died, and the picture he sent of him with "Laura's Guys."

Mr. Martinelli took the Laura's Guys photo and stared at it like it was the first time he had ever seen it.

"Michael was a strong, handsome man. You look so much like him, this could be you in the uniform."

"Thanks."

"How come I no see you in your uniform?"

"Well, you know my mother never married again."

"Yes, I know. Many a man would have liked to marry her."

"All through the rest of her life, she grieved over my father's death. It took a mental toll on her. When I received my ROTC military officer commission, she never acknowledged that I joined the military. So, when I came home on leave, I never wore my uniform, never talked about being in the military, never showed her a photo of me in uniform."

"Yes, Anthony, her broken heart turned her mind from wine to vinegar."

He handed the picture back and asked, *"Coma va,* Anthony?"

"I need your help."

Mr. Martinelli brightened. He liked my answer and looked side to side seeing if anyone was within ear shot. Then he looked at me with an expression that said: 'get on with it'.

"If you see a black Bentley pull up near my place, try to get the license plate number. And, like you always do, let me know if any strangers hang around or go into my flat."

I didn't have to go into details of why. He was already looking up the street to my flat.

"I'll let you know all about it. *Ciao.*"

He wouldn't miss a beat.

"Ciao."

I turned the corner onto Hanover street towards the athletic club. The sun had risen halfway overhead and now provided some welcome heat on a water-freezing day. People walked on the warm side of the street out of the shadows of buildings. A woman approached me with a little boy, maybe four, bundled up in a black parka and knitted beanie. The child was taking two hurried steps to her one. As they walked by, he looked up at me with inquiring brown eyes, and I smiled. As they passed me, he stopped and turned like he wanted to come to me. His mother jerked his hand to keep him walking.

That brief encounter pushed aside the storm clouds that caused my reluctance to marry. I wanted a son, just like him.

Chapter 3

I checked into the gym, rented a towel, and headed to the racquetball court where I ran into Jeff. He was a professional fitness trainer I used once a month so I wouldn't slack off from the fitness level I'd achieved in the military. One could tell he was a bodybuilder, seeing his brawny musculature. With Jeff's assistance, I kept my bench press one max rep at two hundred seventy pounds which was at the "Excellent" level for my 210-pound body weight.

"Good Morning, Mr. April."

"Good morning, Jeff. Appears to be quiet today."

"Monday mornings are usually quiet but, today is unusually quiet. Are we on for Wednesday night?"

"I'm still planning on it, but something has come up which may cause me to cancel. If I do, I'll call."

"No problem. Mr. Berry came in about fifteen minutes ago all puffed up, ready to take you on."

"Thanks for the warning,"

The men's locker room door opened into a small sitting room. No one was in the room, but the television was on.

Around the corner was the dressing room filled with short and tall lockers and long sitting benches. The ever-present odor of sweat-soaked clothes permeated the enclosure.

Bob stood at the far end of the room already dressed to play. He was a sight to behold. *Sports Illustrated* could have used him for an article on "How not to Dress." He was wearing white high-top sneakers that were so worn out the Converse brand name was unrecognizable. Gray socks with red bands on top came almost up to his knees.

His gym shorts were solid red pulled up over a plain white tee shirt that appeared to have been used as a target for bayonet practice. Then he wore a red sweat band on each wrist and one around his bald, shaven head. Cindy, Bob's wife, understood his I-could-care-less attitude about the way he dressed, and always ensured that what he wore was, at least, clean.

At that time, they had four kids, two girls, two boys, and one about two months away. With a salary of $9,800 a year, Bob didn't spend money on clothes.

When I came within speaking distance, he started rocking his five-foot eight-inch gorilla body up and down on his toes.

"April, ready to get your butt beat bad today?"

"What makes you think you can do it today? You got creamed the last time we played."

"Had an off day."

"Hope your knees aren't bothering you today. Get enough sleep last night?" I said.

"Stop talking and get dressed."

"Okay. Hey, Bob, you have time for lunch?"

"Yeah. What's up?"

"I need you to locate a couple of people," I said. "Let's play now and I'll fill you in during lunch."

We played three games. I won the first game, Bob won the second, and we played the third game for lunch. I lost. After the first game, I couldn't clear my mind of the early morning call. It kept playing around in my head.

"Didn't get enough sleep last night, April?"

"I'm wide awake. You just played good."

"Thanks, but after all these years together, I know when something's bothering you."

"Let's shower and go to lunch," I said, not about to minimize his winning the match.

We had lunch in a small restaurant around the corner from the cobblestone plaza that borders Paul Revere's house. The dining room had ten tables, each seating four people. Three of the tables were occupied by two customers each. The walls were plain white plaster worn dull with age. We sat in a far corner of the room away from the only window that fronted the restaurant.

After playing racquet ball, we ate there often. So, Peter, the heavy, demonstrative Italian owner, brought two glasses of Chianti knowing that's what we would have ordered. He spoke to us in English out of courtesy for my Irish companion.

"Good afternoon, gentlemen. By the color in your faces, I see you have played racquet ball."

"I played. Tony just showed up."

Peter knew from Bob's comment who would be paying for lunch, but didn't want to rub it in, so he just asked if were having the usual. Our usual was Italian hot sausage cooked with peppers and onions.

"Yes," we both answered.

"As always, I will make it special for you with some white

wine and oregano. I am going to make some extra for myself."

While Peter was cooking, I went over the early morning's events in detail. Bob sat there stoically listening to each word. When I finished, he remained silent.

"Well?" I asked.

"Well, what?"

"Well, what do you think?"

"I think I beat your butt pretty good today."

"Stop yanking my chain. What do you think?"

"Finding your lady caller will be no problem. When we leave here, we can go over to the station, and I'll call Detective Tim Sweeney out of Weston. He'll know the lady who has a Bentley and a chauffeur named Henry. Finding your Chuck Wilson is going to be more difficult. Your lady caller may or may not know a lot about him. Tell me more about Wilson."

"In August of 1967, I made Captain and was sent from Vietnam to Fort Bragg, North Carolina, for counter-insurgency training of the armies of Latin America. After training, which included high altitude and low opening parachute jumps, along with learning Spanish, I was assigned as a "C" team leader at Fort Gulick in the Panama Canal.

"This was with the 8th Special Forces Group, Special Action Force, Latin America, and Lieutenant Colonel Chuck Wilson commanded my team. He also rotated out of Vietnam to the Panama Canal Zone in 1963 when the United States Army was established at Fort Gulick. He was a sharp-witted, tough commander. We listened and learned from his Vietnam jungle war experience. He never talked about his personal life, and the only clue anyone had about him was the California plates on the Porsche SC90 convertible he drove.

"I assumed he was single since he was a ladies' man. In fact, he introduced me to Bonita which is another story. The Spanish ladies loved the tall, blue-eyed blond American who dressed in expensive civvies, wore a lot of gold jewelry, and spoke Spanish fluently.

"In December, 1969, Wilson introduced us to Lieutenant Colonel Juan Sanchez, as our new 'C' Team Commander and made a brief speech about how proud he was to have served with us and of the way we had performed our missions. He left the meeting and flew out of the base before I had a chance to say goodbye. But, before he left, he said he'd look me up if he ever got to Boston."

"Well, it's obvious he knows where to find you, and that you're a PI, but he didn't contact you directly about the lady caller's problem. Seems like he wants to stay in the background. My guess is that the lady doesn't know much about him. She might not even know how to contact him. Finding her will be no problem if everything we know about her is true. Hopefully, she'll know more about Wilson than I think she does. In the meantime, I'm going to research the Military Personnel Files. Do you know Wilson's full given name?"

"No," I said. "Chuck is the only name I ever knew him by."

"I'll start sorting through the Wilson name with a first or middle name of Charlie, assuming that Chuck is a nickname for Charlie and not a tag for the way he operated. Once I narrow the list down, I'll be able to identify him by records of duty stations and assignments; then, I can go to the National Archives national personnel records. If he has separated from the military, I'll be able to find his home addresses before and after he left the service."

At that point, Peter brought our lunch, the mouthwatering

sausage, peppers and onions smelling as good as the kind my grandmother used to make. Large slices of fresh Italian bread accompanied lunch, and Bob devoured them with gusto. Peter seemed to enjoy Bob's appetite for the bread and always brought two full baskets. It was the only time he would speak to Bob in Italian.

"*Manga,*" he said, with a smile of satisfaction.

I paid the bill, and left a thirty percent tip, which probably only covered the amount of bread Bob consumed. We thanked Peter and walked to the North End police station. After that lunch, the walk felt really good.

The station was a large nineteenth century brick structure with twelve-foot ceilings, windows that rose almost from the floor to the ceiling, and walls painted a light apple green. Bob let the sergeant at the front desk know he'd be in for the rest of the day, and that I was going to his office with him, but wouldn't be staying long. We walked up a flight of stairs to the second floor. Bob's desk was one of ten desks or so placed in a large open space with, of course, green walls. I pulled up a chair on a desk next to Bob and picked up the same phone line to listen to him talk with detective Tim Sweeney.

"Tim, Bob Berry of the Boston Police. How's things?"

"Everything's good. We've been busy investigating the Brinks truck robbery. We found the getaway car, but they torched it, so we haven't lifted any evidence from it yet. What's up, why the call?"

"I have Tony April on the line with me."

"Hi Tony. It's been awhile since the Rayan case."

"Over a year, Tim."

"Tim, we need to locate a woman that supposedly lives in

Weston. I don't know her name, but I understand that she owns a black Bentley and has a chauffeur named Henry. Do you have anyone in town that fits?"

"What's your interest in her?"

"She called Tony about 1:00 a.m. saying it was urgent that she meet with him and that she was sending her chauffeur, Henry, to pick up Tony and bring him to Weston. She hung up without leaving her name or phone number. Then, her chauffeur showed up, but by the time Tony came down from his apartment, both the car and Henry had disappeared."

"That's interesting," said Sweeney.

"What's interesting?" Bob asked.

"Henry's lying in Mass General, unconscious with a brain concussion, and April's lady caller, Barbara Anderson, is in Washington, D.C."

Chapter 4

Bob and I looked at each other in confused silence. From the lull in conversation on our end of the line, Detective Sweeney sensed he'd said something important.

"Did you guys fall asleep?"

"We're trying to digest your information," Bob said.

"I'll read the report: 'Boston called at 2:43 a.m. informing Sergeant Kelley, on desk duty, that a car registered to Barbara Anderson of 2 Willow Road, Weston, had crashed into an abutment at the tunnel entrance to South Station. Henry Willard, also of 2 Willow Road, Weston, was the driver and only occupant. He suffered a head injury and was transported to Mass General.' That's on the written report."

"So, that answers why Henry is in the hospital," I said.

"There's more," Sweeney said. "Henry hitting the abutment wasn't an accident; said he was forced into it. Bob, why not call Captain Rogers, South Boston station. He investigated the crash."

"I know Jack. I'll call him when we're done."

Bob looked at me. "Tony, Henry's bolting out on you, then being forced into the abutment has to be connected."

"I agree."

"Here's some more," Sweeney continued. "'Kelley dispatched officer Reed to the Anderson residence to inform Miss Anderson of the accident and tell her that Henry was in the hospital.' Reed is off duty today, but he's out in the police parking lot tinkering with his car. Do you want me to put him on the phone?"

"Please." Bob said.

"I'm getting off the line. Be prepared, he's a talker."

Officer Reed got on the phone. He was a talker.

"I was patrolling Main Street downtown, when Sergeant Kelley radioed me at zero three twenty-nine hours. He dispatched me to 2 Willow Road, Weston, to inform a Miss Barbara Anderson that her chauffeur had been in an automobile accident and was in Mass General Hospital.

"His injuries weren't critical. I drove up her circular driveway to a beautiful large, white colonial mansion lit up with a dozen outside lights. I parked at the front door, went on the porch, and rang the bell. I rang three times before Miss Anderson came to the door. I heard her tell someone to go back to bed, that she got the door.

"When the door opened, I saw a short, heavy, but not fat, dark haired woman in a bathrobe and slippers going through a door at the end of the foyer. Miss Anderson was fully dressed in a white sweater with black slacks. She's a very attractive woman; had sleepy eyes and was stifling a yawn at 3:36 a.m.

"She asked me to step inside, 'I've been asleep for over two hours,' she told me, 'and was expecting Henry, my chauffeur, to return from the North End two hours ago. Has something happened to him?'

"I told her about the accident and Mr. Willard being in

Mass General. She became very upset and picked up the phone in the foyer. She had a telephone operator connect her to the hospital right away. A doctor on night duty told her that Mr. Willard had regained consciousness, but was presently sleeping. The examination assessment determined that his head injury was minor, and he would probably be released within twenty-four hours.

"She then asked me about the condition of the passenger. I told her I didn't know about any passenger. I was only informed about her chauffeur.

"While she was on the phone, I noticed a suitcase, briefcase, and pair of women's black fur-lined snow boots in the foyer. I asked if she was going somewhere. She said that she was catching a flight from Logan to Washington, D.C., but because she had fallen asleep in the library waiting almost two hours for Mr. Willard, she was now pressed for time and had to meet a scheduled private plane.

"At that point, she called her maid, Gretchen, explained what happened, and asked her to go stay with Mr. Willard. I've never seen an older woman move like a cheetah before, but this one did. Gretchen got dressed, scooped up the suitcase and brief case and was headed for the door. I can only tell you, I was impressed.

"'Gretchen, stop,'" Ms. Anderson called out, 'we don't have a car, call a taxi.' At that point, I told her to wait a minute. I went out to the patrol car and radioed Kelley. He okayed my driving Gretchen to Mass General, and Miss Anderson to Butler Aviation. At Butler an all-white Learjet 24 was already on the lighted tarmac with engines running. I parked next to the access door which immediately opened. The steps came down followed by the co-pilot, with two gold bars on each epaulet. He greeted

Miss Anderson, took her suitcase and briefcase and said, 'You can board now.' Then, he followed her up the stairs and secured the door. The high-pitch engine whined and the wheels started rolling to the runway as the tarmac lights were turned off.

"I love watching aircraft overcome gravity, so I got out of my patrol car and stood on the tarmac sniffing the smell of cold air kerosene. The engines rumbled as the pilot reigned in the beast before releasing all that pent-up energy for her takeoff roll.

"I watched as she rotated to a steep climb into a clear, starlit night, showing off her own red, green, and white lights. It was a thing of pure beauty. In one hour and twenty-four minutes she would be landing in Washington, D.C. You know in the old horse and wagon days, that kind of time would get her just a bit out of Boston."

"Did she tell you why she was going to D.C.?" I asked.

"Said she had an early morning meeting with Admiral Hyman Rickover."

Chapter 5

Bob rolled his chair away from his desk. The conversation with Officer Reed had ended with an amazing revelation. Ms. Andersen was highly connected.

"Let's take a break before we call Captain Rogers. Want a Coke?"

"Sure," I said.

Standing up, I walked around the room to stretch my legs while Bob was getting our drinks. It was 2:45 p.m. Bright sun rays streamed through the windows reflecting off pungent cigarette smoke. The ash trays of two smokers were filled with stubs laying in grey ash. The cigar chewer hadn't fired it up yet. As I walked past, he looked over the top of his *Boston Globe* and said, "Hi." The other two detectives didn't look at me, just kept on writing. I didn't say anything either.

When Bob came in the room with two bottles of Coke, I went back to our desks. We stood, leaning against them, drinking and talking about the Red Sox's spring training in Winter Haven, Florida. Bob put his Coke on his desk and bent over, holding his hands like he was fielding a baseball.

"Can you believe they're paying Luis Aparicio a mammoth thirty-nine grand? He's the highest paid player on the team."

"Well, he was the All-Star game MVP last season," I said.

Bob faked a throw to first and said, "I went into the wrong career."

"Let's call Rodgers," I said.

Bob got ahold of Captain Jack Rodgers and explained our interest in the South Station Tunnel accident. Rodgers sent over a taped interview of Terry Scott, a truck driver from Homestead, Florida, who had witnessed the crash. We listened to the tape:

Scott: My name is Terry Michael Scott. I'm twenty-nine years old from Homestead, Florida; married with two children, both boys. I have an independent trucking business and mainly haul fresh produce to Boston from Florida.

Rodgers: You witnessed the accident?

Scott: Yes, but it wasn't an accident.

Rodgers: What makes you say that?

Scott: I arrived in Boston early and had to wait until 4:00 a.m. to make my first delivery. I parked here, above the expressway, to rest.

Rodgers: Let the record show that Mr. Scott is pointing to a red truck and with a thirty-five-foot white trailer parked on the street next to a six-foot-high brick wall.

Scott: That's my rig. Two years old. The trailer is climate controlled. I didn't want to go to sleep, so I put on my stocking hat and down vest and got out of the truck. I walked over to that railing to look down at the expressway. I lit up a smoke and leaned on the rail. It was cold out, but felt good. The whole city was still, and nothing moved until the I saw the headlights of a car coming down the darkened expressway. It was coming at a good speed heading into the South Station tunnel. The next thing I see and hear is a car with no lights slamming into it, forcing it off the road.

The driver tried to maintain control, but his brakes locked up and he hit the abutment pretty hard. The other car stopped, and two men got out. One ran to the driver's door, opened it, looked in, left the door open, and ran back to his car. The other guy ran to the passenger rear door opened it, removed something, ran back to his car, and they drove off.

I ran to the phone booth over there and had the operator connect me to the Boston Police. I told them an accident had happened, where it happened, and that someone might need medical help. I was trying to find a way down to the expressway when I heard the sirens and saw blue, red and white lights of two police cars, a fire rescue unit, and a fire truck all coming down the expressway.

Rodgers: Can you describe the car that caused the accident?

Scott: I'm sure it was a black Cadillac, but I was too far away to see the license plate.

Rodgers: What did the men look like?

Scott: Again, I was quite a ways off, and the area was pretty dark, except for the car's headlights, which they never walked through. The best I could tell, they were dressed in dark clothes. I'd say one was under six feet, and the other over six.

Rodgers: Thanks for your help Mr. Scott. Do you have a business card in case I need to talk with you again?

The tape ended there. Fire & Rescue had taken the driver to Mass General. Driver was unconscious with a laceration on his forehead. He was identified through his driver's license as Henry Willard of 2 Willow Road, Weston. He was the only occupant in the vehicle. The vehicle, a black 1971 Bentley, is registered to Barbara Anderson of 2 Willow Road, Weston. The car was not drivable at that point and was towed to an impound lot. The identities of the vehicle's owner and driver were called in to the Weston police and recorded at 3:10 a.m., 13 March 1972, by Captain Jack Rodgers.

Bob called Captain Rodgers back saying he had listened to the tape and had obtained permission to talk to Henry Willard. Bob next called the hospital and was told Mr. Willard had regained consciousness and was doing well enough to be interviewed.

We arrived at the hospital around 4:00 p.m. As we walked down the sterile polished corridor to Henry's room, we passed several others with old men lying comatose, tubes sticking out of various parts of their bodies. The place smelled of death. I thought: *Give those guys a break, let them die, disconnect all those frigging plastic tubes.*

When we walked into Henry's private room, I was pleased to see him sitting up in bed, dressed in a hospital gown, watching tv. A white gauze bandage, showing a spot of blood discoloration, was taped to the center of his forehead. A small band-aid taped over the bridge of his nose was bracketed by two puffy black eyes. If he was suffering any pain, he didn't express it.

His driver's license stated he was 60 years old and 5'9". His thick white hair was neatly combed. Henry, apparently, took pride in his head of hair. The black around his eyes didn't mask their light blue color. The muscle tone of his face, neck, and arms showed that he kept himself in good physical shape.

"Good afternoon, Mr. Willard," said Bob. "I'm Detective Bob Berry of the Boston Police Department and this is Tony April, a private investigator. We'd like to ask you a few questions about your accident, if you're up to it."

"I am able, but my hitting the abutment was no accident, I was purposely forced into it after leaving your home, Mr. April."

"Yes, we know it wasn't accidental. A delivery man witnessed you being forced off the road," Bob replied.

"Well, I'm glad there was a witness," Henry said. "Do you know who forced me off the road?"

"No, the witness was too far away to get any information to help us track the vehicle or the men. He did say it appeared to be a black caddy," Bob stated.

"You were parked outside my house, waiting to take me to Weston, and by the time it took me to get ready and come down, you had left. Why did you leave?"

"As I waited for you, a car pulled up behind me. It could have been a black Cadillac. Anyway, two menacing-looking men got out of the car and approached me. One walked to the passenger side, the other came to my side. The one coming to my door appeared to have a gun lowered at his side. I sped away before they could reach me. I saw them in the rearview mirror run back to their car, but I didn't see them follow me. I got on the Southeast Expressway to return to Weston, and the last thing I remember is a car slamming into me, forcing me into the abutment."

"Did you get a good look at the men who approached you?" Bob asked.

"No. I was parked under a streetlight and the reflection of the light off the exhaust from my car made it difficult to see. But they didn't appear to be too tall. The one coming to the passenger side was heavy, maybe even fat. He was wearing a dress hat. The other guy had no hat. If I saw them again, I wouldn't be able to identify them."

"The witness said two men did get out of the car that forced you off the road. One went to your door, opened it, looked in, and returned to his car. The other man went to the rear passenger door and appeared to remove some sort of a package. What was in the back seat that they were so interested in?" Bob asked.

"The only thing in the back seat was a *National Geographic* magazine that Miss Barbara put in the car for Mr. April to read."

"Did her trip to Washington have anything to do with her urgently wanting to see me?"

"I don't know. She tried to contact you all weekend."

"Mr. Willard, how long have you worked for Miss Anderson?" Bob asked.

"I've worked for the family for twenty-seven years. After graduating from high school, in May, 1942, I enlisted in the Marines. On July 1st, 1944, during the battle for Saipan, a bullet caught my left hip. After recovery stateside, I was assigned to General Douglas Smith's personal staff as his driver.

"In October, 1946, two days before I was to muster out, the General sent me to Weston to pick up Mrs. Frances Anderson, Miss Barbara's mother, and bring her to Fort Devens. Mrs. Frances was a psychologist and was helping soldiers transition to civilian life. She had graduated from Wellesley College with a degree in psychology. Normally, she would have driven herself out to the Fort, but had suffered an eye injury. She enjoyed being chauffeured by me to Devens and hired me as her personal driver on the day I left the service.

"Mrs. Frances died five months ago. She was a kind, generous woman. I was with her for over twenty-seven years, and miss her very much. She had a great sense of humor and was a wonderful storyteller.

"Now I drive Miss Barbara. Mrs. Frances had set up a more than enough retirement fund for me, but I would never willingly leave Miss Barbara. She's as kind and generous as her mother was, but more reserved, and analytical.

"Her father was a Biomedical engineer. She was just fourteen when he died of pancreatic cancer. After his death, Mrs. Frances insisted that Ms. Barbara's stay with her. Now that Mrs. Frances has passed, Miss Barbara started talking about completing aspirations she has had since she was a child. The one most important thing to her is finding her grandfather, Dr. George Anderson who disappeared in Ecuador around 1900.

"Dr. Anderson was a biologist and had written research papers on plant cures for yellow fever which Ms. Barbara had read growing up. She was so fascinated by his work that she attained a Ph.D. in Biology several years ago.

"She wants to recover her grandfather's remains and bury him with the rest of the family. She flew a Senor Roberto Sanchez from Ecuador to Weston for the weekend because he had information about the disappearance. She wants your help, Mr. April, and had hoped you would've been available to meet with him before he went back to Ecuador."

"Henry did you see anyone following you while you were driving to my apartment?" I asked.

"I don't think those men followed me. I was parked for a good ten minutes in front of your place before they pulled up behind me."

"You came directly from Logan Airport to my apartment?"

"Yes. I dropped Senor Sanchez off at the Logan Hilton Hotel, then Miss Barbara called and said you were home, gave me your address, and asked me to bring you to Weston."

"You have a radio phone in your car?" I asked.

"Yes."

"Did you tell anyone that you were picking up Mr. April?" Bob asked.

"No, I took Señor Sanchez directly to the Hilton at Logan. He had a flight back to Ecuador in the afternoon and preferred to stay at the hotel since Ms. Barbara was leaving for Washington at 4:30 a.m."

"Is Sanchez a family friend? Bob asked.

"No, I don't believe so. The first time I met him was when I picked him up at the airport two days ago."

"The only purpose of his visit had to do with Miss Barbara's missing grandfather?"

"Yes."

Bob turned and looked at me. I knew what he was thinking. We needed to talk to Miss Anderson as well as the telephone company.

While Bob was thanking Henry and wishing him well, the room phone rang. Henry answered and from the conversation, we could tell Miss Anderson was on the other end. He assured her that he was fine and expressed dismay at wrecking her car. We could tell she was thankful Henry was all right, and telling him the car could be replaced.

"The doctor is keeping me here one more night," Henry told her. She responded that she'd visit him later that evening as soon as she returned to Boston.

"Mr. April and a detective Bob Berry are in the room with me."

Henry handed me the phone. "Miss Barbara would like to speak with you."

"Hello, April here,"

"Hello, Mr. April. Were you also hurt in the accident?"

"No, I wasn't in the car. It's a long story, and I'll fill you in when we meet. When will you be back?"

" I'll arrive at Butler Aviation around seven tonight. Can you met me there, and take me to the hospital?"

"I'll be there,"

"Good, will you give me back to Henry, please?"

I did, then Bob and I waved goodbye to Henry as he returned to the phone call.

It was 4:30 p.m. when we left the hospital. Bob had to go back to his office, and we agreed to get together again after I met with Miss Anderson.

There were a couple of hours to kill before I went to the airport, so I had Bob drop me off at Ellen's workplace. Since my encounter with the little boy, my reluctance to have a family had evaporated and I intended to talk to Ellen about us getting married.

There was only a slight problem: A lightning bolt must have also hit Ellen, but not in the same way. She didn't even give me a chance to propose.

Chapter 6

Ellen worked for a maritime lawyer. I never wanted to utter the fat slob's name. He looked like a walrus always trying to mate with her. I couldn't stand the guy.

As I walked into the reception area, Ellen was standing on a ladder putting books up on a shelf. I looked at her more closely than I had in a long time. Her light blonde hair was pulled back behind her ears exposing small silver drop earrings. Her dress was hiked well above her knees displaying smooth, shapely legs that added to her sex appeal.

She looked down at me with tight lips and squinted eyes.

"What are you doing here?"

"I've got a couple of hours before I need to go to the airport, and I thought I'd see if you wanted to go to dinner. It's almost five."

"I can't. I have a date."

Now, I'm steamed. It's been less than twenty-four hours since our spat, and already she has a date. I can only guess with who.

"So, Fatso finally gets to take you out. I hope you don't kiss the slob goodnight."

I could hear Fatso talking on the phone behind his closed office door.

"Be quiet. Leave, and don't call me."

I didn't have to be asked twice. I had built the guillotine; now she released it and chopped my head off.

I went to Anthony's Pier Four. The working crowd hadn't arrived yet; there were still some tables. I took a couple bottles of Schlitz beer to an empty table in a far corner of the bar and sulked. Ellen, like most women who end relationships, cast me out somewhere in space like I never existed in her life

People started to file in, and the waitress came to see if I wanted anything. I said no, paid the check, and left for the airport.

It was 6:40 p.m. when the white Learjet 24 appeared out of a night sky bright with full moon and millions of twinkling stars. It taxied onto the lighted tarmac and came to a halt with its passenger door facing the terminal entrance. I had parked to the side of the small wooden terminal and rolled my fogged window down to let in crisp winter air.

The jet engines wound down to silence, and the smell of unburned kerosene jet fuel filled the air. The stairs slowly extended. One pilot walked part-way down before turning to help Miss Anderson exit. They were followed by another crew member who carried her suitcase and briefcase.

I got out of my car to walk over and greet her. I was enchanted. Doctor Zhivago was the best romantic movie I had ever seen, and Miss Anderson struck me as the beautiful actress, Phyllis Dalton, except with dark eyes and dark hair. She wore a fur hat with a maxi-military style coat, and black leather boots. From Henry's description of her, I was expecting a conservatively-dressed analytical woman, not the elegant lady I was looking at now.

I stopped outside of hearing distance as she spoke to the two pilots. When they finished, she turned to me.

"Mr. April?"

"Yes."

I reached for her luggage, and she nodded permission for the pilot to release it. Then, not wearing coats, the pilots were more than happy to retreat inside the plane away from the frigid north wind.

"Do you have to go inside?"

"No, everything is taken care of."

"Then, I'll get my car. It's parked on the side of the terminal building."

"Thank you, but I'll walk with you, if you don't mind."

I am liking this woman. She has some spunk.

My car wasn't as roomy as a Bentley, but, as much as she was bundled up, she easily slid inside without complaint.

"Mr. April, had I known Henry hadn't picked you up, I would have followed up with a phone call. My sincere apologies for not identifying myself or giving you my number. I did, however, call you several times from Washington today, but got no answer."

"I was out all day tracking you down."

"I'm impressed you found me."

I just looked at her and smiled, not responding, just thinking to myself, *I wish I had found you a long time ago.*

She suggested we first visit Henry at the hospital, then go to her home for dinner, which Gretchen, her live-in domestic, would prepare.

"We can discuss what services I need from you."

I agreed without hesitation...

Henry was sitting up in bed when we arrived; we stayed about half an hour, long enough for him to tell of his recollection of events leading up to being forced off the road. I added Scott's eyewitness account including the fact that one of the men took something from the back seat of the Bentley.

"Henry told me you put a *National Geographic* magazine on the back seat of the Bentley for me to read." She was quiet for a brief moment.

"I'm surprised at their extent of violence for the magazine," she said. "By now they know the copy I put in the car isn't the one they want. We best save that discussion for cocktail hour."

I could see she was tired, so didn't press for an explanation.

As we got ready to leave, Miss Anderson clasped Henry's hands and expressed how thankful she was that he was not severely injured. She told him his doctor had approved his discharge in the morning, and for him to drive. She would, therefore, have the Bentley dealer deliver a loaner car to the hospital for him to use while the damaged one was being repaired. Henry was all smiles. He was back chauffeuring for Miss Barbara.

The drive to Weston took a little over thirty-five minutes. All roads were clear on the Massachusetts Turnpike following a snow that had fallen the day before. Traffic was light for a Friday night, as was the conversation. But I did learn how she came to contact me.

"Mr. April, I understand that you served in the Army Special Forces with Colonel Chuck Wilson."

"Yes, we served a tour of duty together at Fort Gulick in the

Panama Canal Zone, but I haven't seen or heard from him, nor known his whereabouts, since he shipped out of the Zone five years ago."

"Well, he certainly knows a lot about you. He gave me your phone number, address, and your occupation as a private investigator."

"Oh."

"I'm surprised that he has not been in touch with you for five years. However, I am not surprised that he knows so much about you presently, since he works for the National Security Agency."

"Oh." Was all I said until I cleared my musing." "How did the two of you meet?"

"I was at a meeting in Washington, D.C., at the request of Admiral Rickover's staff to provide any information that my grandfather, George Anderson, may have recorded on the day the battleship USS Maine was destroyed in 1898. My grandfather was well-known to keep a meticulous diary, and the Admiral knew he had been onboard the Maine prior to its explosion. After the meeting, Colonel Wilson approached me and volunteered to help in the search for my grandfather's remains. He recommended I call you since you had made many sorties into the Ecuadorian mountains while stationed in the Panama Canal Zone."

"When I see him again, I'll thank him for the endorsement."

We sat in silence for most of the remaining trip to Weston. Starring out the window, I was absorbed in thought about all she had told me.

My big question: Exactly, what does she expect from me?

Her residence was impressive by the grounds alone. A quarter mile-long driveway carpeted with two inches of snow was lined with tall, naked oak trees. It led to a large, two-story white Georgian-style home with black shutters facing south. Tall pines lined the back of the house helping block the north winter winds. The house retained two colonial Tory chimneys colored white with black bands, once a secret sign the house was occupied by British loyalists. Alongside a road branching off the circular drive, was a two-story, white cottage, a dark red carriage house, and a large barn.

The light from the full moon glistened off the snow-covered grounds, except where shadowed by buildings and trees. The scene brought me back to an era of candlelight and horse carriages. Later, I learned that her home was over 200 years old and had gone through several interior restorations.

Gretchen answered the clang of the doorbell and warmly welcomed Miss Barbara back home. She was wearing a frilly black and white maid's dress and black shoes with low heels. A white-hooped gothic hairband held back her graying black, shoulder-length hair. She was heavy, but muscular, and spoke with a thick Irish brogue. It was easy to see how protective Gretchen was of Miss Anderson. I wouldn't want her coming at me with a cast-iron frying pan if she felt threatened. Gretchen ignored me until Miss Anderson introduced me as a friendly visitor. Then, took our coats and hats and the overnight suitcase. Miss Anderson kept the briefcase.

"Miss Barbara, I stayed overnight with Henry last night. I knew he wasn't hurt bad by his usual teasing. After you called that you were coming to the hospital, I left. Are you and Mr. April having dinner?"

"Please."

"Dinner will be ready in twenty minutes," Gretchen said heading for the kitchen door at the end of the foyer.

Looking after her, I saw how wide and long the hallway seemed with a floor covered in black and white foot-square marble tiles. To the right was a beautifully gleaming, varnished oak banister that curved up the stairway leading to the second floor.

Opposite the stairs was a door to the library, and beyond the stairs, to the right side of the foyer, was the formal dining room. Past the foyer, I would later learn, were the rest of the rooms including a kitchen and smaller dining room, Gretchen's bedroom, and two bathrooms. Henry lived in the small white cottage I'd seen on the grounds when we arrived.

"That's fine, Gretchen," Miss Anderson called after her. "We'll be in the library. I'll have a glass of red wine." Gretchen stopped and waited. "What would you like Mr. April?"

"Red wine, also."

"Is a California cabernet sauvignon suitable?"

"Yes, thanks."

"Two glasses of my usual red wine, please, Gretchen."

Miss Anderson led the way into the library. It appeared to be of medium size, but I couldn't see its features hidden in the shadows since the room was dark and lit only by a crackling fire. I sensed this was Miss Anderson's favorite realm. We sat on firm, wingback chairs which faced each other by the fireplace. A glass coffee table was set between us.

As we settled into the comfortable chairs, Gretchen entered with two long-stemmed glasses on a silver serving tray filled with aromatic red wine. She placed the tray on the coffee table and left the room. We picked up our glasses with nods of welcome, then Miss Anderson turned her head and stared into the flames dancing in the fireplace. In seconds, her mind was lost in thought.

A moment later, she said, "I apologize, Mr. April, my mind wandered off. It has been a busy day for both of us, hasn't it."

"Yes, it has."

"Mr. April, I am tired, and I assume you are as well. I woke you at 1:00 a.m. and asked you to come here because it was urgent. Now the urgency has passed. However, the five thousand dollar bribe I offered you to meet still stands. If you decide to take me on as a client, we will discuss your ongoing fees.

"I can tell that you have been restraining yourself from asking questions, but the answers will take time, and I am not up for it tonight. I suggest that we have a pleasant dinner, you stay here tonight, and tomorrow I will be ready for your inquiry. What say you, Private Sleuth April?"

"I'll stay," I smiled, man of few words that I am.

Addressing me as "Private Sleuth April" told me she was really tired. I had no problem with staying overnight, either since I wasn't crazy about driving back to the North End this late.

But before going into dinner, I wanted to check the phone on her desk. I was pretty sure it was tapped. How else would someone know that she'd instructed Henry to pick me up, and at what address? However, something told me to hold off until morning.

"Your home and its setting want to reveal their history. I can almost hear the walls talk."

"You're very perceptive," she said. "The property has been owned by my family for nearly two-hundred years. My great-great-grandfather, George Ashton, acquired it during the Revolutionary War from a family that supported the British and fled to Canada. Although the home has gone through several restorations, this room, like most of the house, has remained nearly untouched since the seventeen-hundreds. The workmanship is superb.

"When I was a little girl, my father would bring me into this room and sit with me in front of a blazing fire, just as we are seated tonight. He would turn off the lights, so I could feel the spirit of this room, and what it was like when my great-great grandfather and his wife, Ashley, would sit here talking about their eight children, and news of the Revolutionary War. Father would recount some of the things they might have said while mimicking Ashton's voice. My father died seventeen years ago. You can imagine how this room is a special place for me."

Sorrowfully, she added that since both her parents were gone, she was the last of the Anderson line at just thirty-one years old, and childless.

"Have you any favorite childhood memories, Mr. April?" she asked, trying to brighten her mood a little.

"My grandfathers and grandmothers all came to America from Italy, but never talked to me about their parents. It seemed, when they came to America, they wanted to leave their memories and history of Italy behind. My paternal grandfather, Pasquale Aprille, even changed his last name to April. He was the male influence in my life after my father was killed while serving in the Army Air Corp in World War Two. I was only four years old.

"Patsy, as they called him, didn't have a formal education beyond the third grade, but he was a skilled stone mason. While other men would pound repeatedly on a boulder to split it, Patsy could split it with one well-placed whack. When I was strong enough to lift a ten-pound sledgehammer, he taught me how to read a stone's structure, and, as I got older, I helped him by splitting boulders on construction jobs.

"At night we would press home-grown juicy red grapes to

make wine or sit dunking fresh Italian bread into a glass of red wine, then eating the bread and drinking the wine. He limited me to one small glass a day. We talked a lot together. His favorite subject was school, but I always learned a lot just listening to him on any day.

"Patsy loved to eat rabbit, and when I was twelve years old, he gave me a ten-gauge shotgun. Not a good gun for hunting rabbit, but that was all he had. Anyway, my friend, Joe, and I would take a twenty-mile bus ride from Lawrence to Haverhill and hunt along the railway tracks back to Lawrence. We had to walk through downtown Lawrence to get to Patsy's house. Two kids with shotguns and rabbits hanging from their belts evoked smiles from people or a comment about what good hunters we were. It was a different world then.

"At sixteen, I was skinny, six feet tall, and quite strong. I decided to try club fighting. Men's clubs would bring in so-called boxers to entertain their members. No special training or qualifications were required, just come and fight and get beat up, and earn two bucks. My one and only fight lasted thirty seconds. At the time, I didn't know I was about to fight an amateur champion. The bell rang and we met in the center of the ring. Before I got my gloves up, he must have hit me fifty times. So, I applied my street fighting skills. I grabbed his left arm, kicked his legs out from under him, and jumped on top of him. I was thinking of giving him a shot to the head when the ref and another guy pulled me off and threw me out the door. I waited for the kid outside and apologized. Now, he's my best friend, Boston police detective Bob Berry. You'll meet him soon."

As I finished my story, Gretchen came in to say that dinner was ready. We left our empty glasses and strolled to an informal dining room which was sparsely furnished with a sturdy rectangular oak table and eight chairs, a cupboard, and a fireplace that popped gas pockets in burning oak logs. The floor was made of natural wide pine board, and the walls were covered with dark walnut embossed wood.

When we were seated, Gretchen poured another two glasses of red wine and went back to the kitchen. She returned with a tray bearing small Caesar salads, plates of tangy veal piccata, and fresh Italian bread. The smell of the lemon piccata sauce piqued my appetite, as I felt ravenously ready to eat.

All through dinner we talked about current world events, had a snifter of Cointreau after dinner, then retired to separate rooms. On the guest room bed was a bathrobe, pajamas, towels, and a note: 'Leave clothes you want washed outside your door. Breakfast will be served at eight. Barbara.'

I took a shower, and even though I was tired, had a hard time relaxing. My mind would not stop trying to put the pieces of the puzzle together. Breakfast would be served at eight, and I anticipated that Barbara would be ready to talk about the circumstances that caused her to seek my services. Exhaustion finally won and I fell asleep.

Chapter 7

Morning sunlight glimmering through bedroom windows woke me at 6:30 a.m. Taking a few moments to orient myself to the unfamiliar setting, pleasant memories flowed through my mind of the evening with Miss Anderson.

From my second-floor bedroom window, I could see the cottage, carriage house, and barn nearby, and in the distance, chimney smoke coming from a white Colonial house. In the foreground was an apple orchard with unpicked apples, now frozen, yet still hanging from many branches. Snow was marked by fresh cross-country ski tracks which had been made by Miss Anderson, I later learned at breakfast.

When I peeked out my door, I found clean clothes and a *National Geographic* magazine, lying on the carpet with a note attached.

"If you have time before breakfast, please read the article starting on page 22. Barbara." That was the beginning of our informal relationship.

After I shaved and showered, there was still forty minutes before breakfast to read the article. It began with the discovery of quinine being the most effective cure for the diseases of malaria and yellow fever. Quinine was extracted from the bark of cinchona trees which grew in the treacherous Llanganates mountains of Ecuador, making it difficult to obtain an adequate supply to cure the multitude of infected Panama Canal construction workers.

In February,1897, *National Geographic* funded a proposal by botanist Dr. George Anderson to go to the Llanganates and bring back Cinchona saplings and seeds for cultivation in the United States.

Dr. Anderson sailed out of Boston Harbor on February 1, 1898, on the two-masted schooner, *Adventurer,* with Captain McGee and four crew. They anchored in Havana Harbor, Cuba, on February 14th, intending to stay for two days in order to bring on fresh supplies.

The very next night, the battleship *USS Maine,* anchored just 400 yards away, exploded, and a projectile of armored plate sheared off the top of the *Adventurer's* foremast. No one onboard the *Adventurer* was hurt, but it took two days to get the schooner fit enough to limp into Colon, Nicaragua, where repairs took another six weeks

Captain McGee and Jonathan Barn, a ten-year-old cabin boy, stayed with the vessel to oversee repairs. The rest of the expedition crossed the Isthmus of Panama by rail to Balboa, and from there, traveled by boat to northern Ecuador, then overland by horseback to the city of Quito. They planned to be back in Colon within eight weeks.

Before reading on, I looked at several black and white pictures. One showed the six expedition members as they posed alongside the schooner docked in Boston Harbor. Another showed the damaged *Adventurer.* A third photo was a close-up of Dr. Anderson and his Ecuadorian guide with the inscription:

"Ecuadorian Inca guide, Juan Sanchez, and Dr. Anderson."

The last photo showed the expedition members and their burdened pack horses, along with a note written by Dr. Anderson:

"Leaving for the Llanganates, February 20, 1898. Will not be able to provide any more news until I emerge from the mountains. I will keep a detailed day-by-day record in my diary."

That was the last communication *National Geographic,* or anyone else, ever received from the expedition. *National Geographic* searched for over a year, but no trace of the expedition was ever found.

I heard a Westminster clock chime to the strike of eight. It was time for breakfast. When I reached the informal, bright breakfast room, furnished with a small wooden table and four chairs, there was a peaceful view of white, fluffy snow covering the apple orchard outside the window. Gretchen was setting a pitcher of orange juice on the table.

"Good morning, Gretchen,"

"Good morning, Mr. April. Would you like coffee?"

"Not yet, thanks. I'll wait for Miss Anderson,"

"She's on the phone. She'll be right in. *The Boston Globe* is in the library. Would you like me to get for you?"

"No thanks," I didn't want Gretchen to disturb Barbara's phone call.

Sitting down to ponder *National Geographic's* chronicle of Dr. Anderson's lost expedition, I read the belief that Anderson must be buried in the Llanganates. Maybe this was the reason Wilson, an NSA agent. had suggested that Barbara hire me to help find the doctor's remains. I later learned that everyone had an interest in Dr. Anderson's diary: Admiral Rickover's group investigating the sinking of the *Maine* wanted it. The NSA wanted to destroy it. Barbara wanted it for sentimental reasons.

Her grandfather was on board the *Maine* hours prior to it being destroyed. He had tried to inform the 1898 Board of Inquiry about the suspicious actions of the visitor in front of him. They had ignored him. The Board didn't want to hear any evidence that could disprove their claim that the *USS Maine* was absolutely destroyed by Spain.

In 1972, Admiral Rickover started an investigation into what actually caused the explosion of the *Maine*. He knew that Spain didn't want to go to war with the U.S. and had placed blame for the sinking of the ship on a "false flag". That possibility was bolstered by the false flag war with Vietnam, and the Pentagon's "Operation Northwood's Proposal" in which thirteen false flag actions were submitted to President Kennedy in order to validate going to war with Cuba. Their proposal included the sinking of a U.S. warship in Guantanamo Bay. But, in the end, the President vetoed all their proposals.

However, President Johnson was led to declare war on Vietnam because apparently Vietnamese torpedo boats had attacked the destroyers *Maddox* and *Turner Joy*, even though these were later found to be real false flags.

I concluded that Wilson had brought me into the search for Dr. Anderson's grave believing that if the diary was found, he could convince me to destroy it. The NSA would be deeply troubled if Dr. Anderson's diary was given to Rickover. If his investigation found that the sinking of the *Maine* was a false flag, the credibility of the NSA would then come into question.

I was in the process of pouring another cup of coffee, when Gretchen returned.

"Ms. Barbara is off the phone and will be right in. I am going to start breakfast. Do you like eggs Benedict Mr. April?"

"Very much."

"You must be favored by Miss Barbara for her to have me cook special for you. She hasn't had a life of her own since her father died seventeen years ago. Mrs. Francis insisted that Miss Barbara remain by her side up until she died, three months ago. I am so pleased that she is now getting on with her life."

Just as Gretchen was about say something else, Barbara walked in, and Gretchen hastily left for the kitchen. This was the first time I had seen her in daylight, and she was beautiful. Her athleticism showed right through the ski clothes she wore: a white turtleneck under a black and white Nordic sweater and black ski pants. Her high cheekbones glowed a healthy, slightly pinkish tone.

"Good morning. You've been outside," I said.

"Good morning. Yes, I have. I went out at six and cross-country skied three miles. I enjoy getting out at dawn and feeling the beginning of a new day."

"Would you believe, most days, I am out at dawn running five miles?"

"Do you cross-country ski?" she asked.

"A couple of times, but I'm really a downhill skier."

Gretchen came in and placed a perfectly assembled dish of eggs Benedict in front of me covered with a creamy pale-yellow hollandaise sauce and sliced tomatoes on the side. She filled our coffee cups, poured two glasses of orange juice.

"Enjoy your breakfast," she said and left.

"Mr. April, may I call you Tony?

"I would be pleased."

"Have you ever skied Tuckerman Ravine? You appear to be the type of man that would attempt it."

"I did once, but it wasn't pretty. I ended up at the bottom, destroyed. No skis, one ski pole, no hat, googles full of snow, but no broken bones. Do you downhill?"

"Yes. I wanted to do Tuckerman, but my father said no. We had a chalet at the bottom of Mount Washington. We would hike Tuckerman and to the top of Washington at least twice a year."

"Well, I'm impressed. The hike up is demanding."

"Dad was an avid outdoorsman, and gave me the discipline to plan, and survive, anticipated dangers. My training will serve me well when I go to the Llangantes mountains to look for my grandfather."

I stopped eating. Apparently, she meant what she'd said. I could see by her gaze that she was trying to read my reaction to her declaration.

"Barbara, the Llanganates mountains are deadly; it's not like Mount Washington. People die, and are never found again."

"Tony, a lot of people have died on Washington, too, and some are never found."

"That's true, but the Presidential Mountain Range is a walk in the park compared to the Llanganates. I know, because I hiked the Presidential and crawled the Llanganates."

"Well, that's the reason I hired you."

"First, I didn't know I was hired. Secondly, we haven't discussed my fee. And thirdly, I don't even know what you want from me."

Her expression told me everything had already been decided, but what she said was, "Tony, after breakfast, let's go to the library and I'll answer all your questions."

Chapter 8

Barbara and I reconvened to the library. Unlike my visit the previous night, I could see the entire room and its furnishings this morning because the room was lit with sunshine. The back wall of the classroom-sized library was lined with three-tiered shelves, all stacked with books. The top shelf held thick brown-bound medical books, some published more than a century ago. In front of the shelves a double-pedestaled cherry wood desk supported a phone, lamp, pen set, open notebook, and family pictures.

A black leather desk chair was rolled against the bookshelves; it had arms and a mid-level back. Two tall windows on the wall facing the driveway were decorated with heavy tan drapes pulled open to let in the light. A wide red brick fireplace was built into the right wall and was crackling with the smell of burning oak logs.

We settled into burgundy-colored leather wingback chairs by the fireplace. The coffee table between the chairs had been set with a pitcher of ice water and two glasses. A fresh log looked like it had just been added to the fireplace. Gretchen was on top of everything. Barbara began the conversation.

"Did you read the *National Geographic* article?"

"Yes, I did."

"Dr. George Anderson was my grandfather."

"I assumed he was."

"He was in Havana Harbor the night the *Maine* blew up. It seems he had taken a tour of the ship during that very day and wrote this letter to his wife about the visit."

Barbara handed me a faded letter dated February 16, 1898. Flickering flames from the fireplace made reading difficult, so I turned on the floor lamp beside my chair.

Dearest Eleanor,

We arrived in Havana, Cuba, on the morning of 14 February. Captain McGee and I had plans to go to Havana in the afternoon but were discouraged from doing so. The crew member of a passing boat told us of dire conditions in the city: "Fifty Reconcentrados a day are dying from starvation or malaria and are being thrown into a field unburied. There are also 33,000 Spanish soldiers sick with fever." This situation is beyond our understanding, so we did not go for fear of the affliction.

The next day a most unexpected tragedy happened. Captain McGee and I were sitting on deck enjoying a pleasant warm evening. Our ship, The Adventurer, was anchored about three cable lengths from the battleship USS Maine. In an instant, the dark evening was changed into misfortune as the Maine exploded in flames and quickly sank with the loss of 265 men. The vessel blew up near 10 p.m. Imagine, I had been aboard the Maine that very afternoon! Spain was immediately blamed for the destruction, saying they planted a mine in the harbor. But, to tell you the truth, my dear, I doubt the cause was a Spanish mine. I was more suspicious of a man who walked in front of me during my tour of the ship. He held a cigar-shaped object in his right hand, and when he took his turn to view the coal storage area, he sheltered his eyes with his hands as he looked through the inspection port. When he turned away, his hand was empty. Whatever he had held in his hand, I am sure he dropped into the coal bunker. Most strange behavior.

We are leaving tomorrow morning for Colon, Nicaragua, for repairs to the Adventurer as it has received debris damage from the explosion. American authorities have blindly accused Spain for the sinking, totally ignoring eyewitness observations that refute the cause being a Spanish mine. I have written details of my observations, and the man's name, in my diary. Upon my return from Ecuador, I will attempt to have a hearing with the Board of Inquiry. Perhaps by then, they will be more open to considering other alternatives that might have caused the explosion than just a Spanish mine.

The days since we have parted are few, but already it seems like an eternity. Give little George a big hug for me, and I, pray God, will be home by June for his birthday.

I must close now to get this letter on the mail boat.

Your Loving Husband, George

"Now I understand why Wilson cares whether you find your grandfather. The diary is most likely with him, and if it's found, they will want to make sure it never sees the light of day."

"Why is that?"

"Currently, NSA's usefulness is under question for not identifying the false flag that helped start U.S. involvement in the Vietnam war. They will withhold any evidence from Rickover which might help conclude that NSA also failed to identify a false flag that helped start a war with Spain, even as far back as 1898."

Barbara eyes narrowed, "They would do that?"

"There are bad guys in high places that will do anything to save their butts. Did you give this letter to Rickover's staff?" I asked while handing her the letter. She put it on her lap.

"No. I only sent a copy to Chuck Wilson."

"Why Wilson?"

"Six weeks ago, I received a call from Wilson, and he identified himself as an agent for the National Security Agency. He said he was helping with Admiral Rickover's inquiry into the sinking of the battleship *Maine* and was aware that my grandfather had witnessed the sinking. He was seeking any additional information that my grandfather might have passed on to his family.

"At the time, I hadn't gone through grandfather's papers, yet, and said I had nothing. He gave me his phone number and asked me to call if something did turn up. He was very pleasant and expressed condolences on the disappearance of my grandfather, and the recent death of my mother. For someone I'd never met, I was surprised he knew so much about me, where I lived, and especially that my mother had recently died."

"Now, you're on his radar," I said, "You've forgotten more details about your life than the National Security Agency has probably uncovered."

She picked the letter off her lap. "When I found this letter, I called Mr. Wilson and sent him a copy. A few days later he called asking many questions about diaries: 'Had I seen or found any of my Grandfather's diaries?' No. 'Did my father or mother keep a diary?' No. 'Did I know the name of the man on the tour that your Grandfather observed acting suspiciously?' No. 'Did I keep a diary myself?' 'No, but I've started to keep a one now as I am preparing to look for my grandfather's remains in Ecuador,' I blurted out before saying goodbye.

"In less than an hour he called back, 'Miss Andersen, if you're going to search for your grandfather's remains in the Llanganates mountains, you will need assistance. I can recommend a former special forces soldier who knows the dangerous Llangantes mountains. He's physically tough, intelligent, and speaks Spanish. His named Tony April.'"

Barbara raised her eyebrows and said with an impish smile, "Do you know a Tony April?"

"Most of the time."

"He gave me your phone number and address, about ten days ago, but I hesitated to call you. Now, although I've known you for less than twenty-four hours, I feel I can trust you."

Her beautiful brown eyes were fixed on me.

"Tony, I must have your word that anything I tell you in confidence will not be passed on to Wilson or anyone else."

"That's a given. You have my word." I was touched by her faith in me.

Barbara poured a glass of water, held the pitcher up over the other glass, and I nodded. We emptied the glasses as she began telling me her confidential information.

"Okay. About two weeks ago, a Senor Roberto Sanchez called, saying he had read the *National Geographic* article and had information about my grandfather's lost expedition. But, he insisted I not share it with anyone. Roberto Sanchez is the son of Paulo Sanchez who guided my grandfather's expedition. His father had possession of a document, he said, that was written in the late fifteen hundreds claiming it would lead to a treasure hidden by the Incas in a valley forested by Cinchona trees. The Cinchona valley was where grandfather wanted to do his research. Roberto indicated the trail to the valley on the map of the Llanganates mountains included in *National Geographic* article. He, then, mailed me the magazine."

"Is that the *National Geographic* you put in the Bentley to for me to read?"

"No, I put in my regular copy of the magazine. Roberto's copy is in this desk."

"Good, they didn't get what they wanted." But how did they know about it, I wondered.

"After talking with Roberto, I considered looking for my grandfather's remains, but before I made a final decision, I flew Roberto here last weekend to meet him. After being with him for two days, I found him to be an intelligent, honest man, and believable. I told him I had decided to search for my grandfather's remains, but had someone in mind to accompany me. Then, I asked him if he would he be willing to meet with you, and he said 'yes'.

"I tried all weekend to get in touch with you. Not being comfortable arranging the meeting before I met you, I insisted you to come to Weston even in the middle of the night. Henry had already taken Roberto to the Logan Hilton near the airport to stay the night before a mid-morning flight back to Ecuador. There would have still been time enough in the morning for the two of you to meet even thought I had to take an early morning flight to Washington.

"Anyway, as you know, everything got messed up, and you two never met. So, this morning, while you were in the breakfast room, I called him in Ecuador. I told him that you could be trusted to keep his information secret. He said he had confidence in my judgement, and it was okay to confide in you."

I abruptly stood up.

"Barbara, before you think I haven't kept my word, I need to check your phone."

"What has my phone got to do with your word?"

I picked up the receiver and heard the telltale static. The phone was tapped from outside the house. Barbara got up and walked next to me.

"What are you doing?"

"Wilson tapped your phone. He has a trust problem with you, and now we have an additional problem."

"Why,"

"In Panama, he always talked about someday looking for the lost Inca gold. Now he'll want the diary and the map to the gold."

Barbara flopped into the desk chair. "You're saying he knows everything Roberto and I talked about over the phone?"

"I assume so. But, when Roberto was here, did he disclose any information that he didn't want to talk about over the phone?"

"Yes," she said, her eyes looking straight into mine.

"Tell me what Roberto doesn't want revealed."

"Paulo Sanchez is alive."

Chapter 9

When Barbara said Paulo Sanchez was still alive, my mind reeled with questions and I went silent. She sat with her hands clasped on her lap staring at me, waiting for me to say something. A loud "pop" from the fireplace jolted me back to the present moment.

"How old is Paulo Sanchez?"

"He's ninety-four."

"You accept Roberto's word that Paulo was the guide?"

"Yes, he gave me this."

Barbara retrieved Roberto's *National Geographic* from a side desk drawer and handed it to me opened to the pictures of the expedition on facing pages. Placed in between the pages was a loose three-by-five-inch black and white photo discolored with age. I noticed it was a duplicate of one printed in the magazine, but had a different notation. The pictures both showed two unsmiling men standing shoulder to shoulder, but while the magazine's caption read, Dr. Anderson and Ecuadorian guide," the loose photo was autographed, 'To Paulo, From Dr. George.'

"Roberto gave you this photo?" I asked.

"Yes. Here's what he told me:

'At the age of ten, I saw Papa take out a wooden cigar box from a wall cavity behind a flat stone in his bedroom where it was hidden. He didn't see me watching. I saw him put *scudos* from a llama sale into the box, then return it into the wall and replace the stone.

'Several days later, I couldn't resist the temptation to look in the box. My father, mother, brother and three sisters were planting corn in the plowed field with me far from the house. I told them I had a stomachache and had to relieve myself. But, instead, I looked back to make sure my family was still in the field, then, went into the bedroom and removed the box from the wall. I opened it, expecting to find some hidden treasure, but all I found was money and a photo of Papa with this gringo. It didn't interest me at the time, so I quickly put the box back.

'When I later saw the same photo in *National Geographic,* I realized that my father was the guide of the lost expedition. He had never revealed what happened to Dr. Anderson and his men.

'Early the next day, I took the magazine and drove home to Cota to see if the photo was still hidden in the wall. To reach the house by car requires an off-road drive for two kilometers uphill over mud and ruts which takes over an hour.

'When I finally arrived, I was greeted by Laka, my Padre's hairless pito dog, who bounded up the road in front of my car wiggling her body and whipping her tail. Isa, my oldest sister, and only one living with Padre, walked up and hugged me while Laka forced herself between our legs. 'She's been waiting for you ever since you started up the hill. Papa is in the kitchen.'

'My brother and I had made some updates to the house by covering the dirt floor with cement, installing a sink with a hand pump that drew water from an outside well, and adding a black cast iron wood burning stove along with an oak table and four chairs. But we could never get rid of the lingering smell of farm animals that used to stay in the house during severe cold weather.

'Isa went to the orchard with Laka to pick naranjllas, small oranges. I went through the back door to Papa's bedroom to find the photo. This time, I took it and the *National Geographic* into the kitchen.

'Papa sat at the kitchen table, with a glass of red wine, fixing shearing scissors. I placed the photo and the opened magazine on the table in front of him. He glanced down at the pictures and went back to fixing the scissors. But I could tell from the way he fumbled with the shears that he was reliving the expedition. But he wasn't about to talk of it. After a deep breath, I said that the pictures proved he guided Dr. Anderson's expedition. Slowly, Padre closed the magazine and remained silent.

'I was frustrated. I yelled that the families of the missing men have suffered for seventy-five years not knowing what happened. I pointed at him and said that he was an old man now and if he died, no one would ever know. Papa's shoulders slumped and his head bowed toward the top of the table. I knew his was pained and bent down to hug him, worried that my lashing out had hurt him. He returned my embrace saying, 'The time has come.' I hugged him harder and kissed his forehead.'"

Barbara took a deep breath. "Roberto wrote down what Paulo revealed to him that day and the story of how he became the expedition guide. He also wrote down why the expedition was lost and why it was never found."

"Do you have a copy?"

She hesitated, "Yes, it's in the desk, I'll get it."

When she returned, she handed me two handwritten pages which I eagerly read:

At seventeen years old, I left Cota for work in Quito. On that day, while walking up Quito Mountain, a stranger met me and asked if I walked the mountains often. I told him, "Yes, I live in the mountains, and am going to Quito to look for work." He said his name was Diego Ramos Cruz, owner of a guide business, and that I looked strong and healthy. He needed porters for an expedition into the Llanganti and offered me seven scudos a day, so I said I would work for him.

Over the next year, I worked as a porter, and Diego taught me the ways to organize and guide an expedition. Diego planned to go back to Spain and wanted me to take over his guide business.

I helped Diego put together his last expedition for a client named Mr. Green who was seeking a lost Incan village. Mr. Green owned a gold mine in California and came a few days before we left for the Llanganti. He was a big man with gray hair and loud voice, but he always talked muffled to Diego. Even so, when all was ready, we set out on the expedition.

On the twenty-fourth day, as we were deep in the mountains, Mr. Green did not come to breakfast. Diego went to wake him, but Mr. Green was not in his tent. Diego searched for him all morning but never found him. Mr. Green had vanished. When Diego came back to camp without Mr. Green, we all knew that Green was really seeking Atahualpa's gold, not a lost Incan village. We hurried to leave before we would be as lost as the doomed expedition.

Diego asked me to keep the porters together and take them to Spectacle Lake where the horses were waiting. We should remain there while he stayed to look for Mr. Green. He promised to search for two days, and if Mr. Green was found alive, they would join us at the lake where he would try to get the porters back to work. If he didn't find

Mr. Green, he would still join us but return the expedition to Quito and pay the porters.

As I turned the next page Barbara interrupted my thoughts.

"While you were in Ecuador, did anyone ever talk about the Incan treasure?"

"Once, after a few beers, when Carlos, an Inca Ecuadorian soldier, and I sat alone by the glow of a blazing campfire in the Llangantes, I asked if he believed the Incan treasure was somewhere in the mountains. Carlos said he knew the Incan treasure was in the mountains, but a curse had been put on anyone seeking it.

"The flames of the fire reflected in his wide eyes as he spoke, 'The curse was placed as a result of the broken word of Francisco Pizarro, the Spanish conquistador who captured and imprisoned the Incan Emperor Atahualpa. Atahualpa had offered to fill Pizarro's prison cell with gold for his freedom. Pizarro agreed to the bargain, at first, but reneged on his promise and had Atahualpa garroted and burned at the stake. The word of Atahualpa's execution reached Incan General Ruminahui who was on his way to Cajamarca with tons of gold. Ruminahui diverted the gold to the treacherous and unforgiving wilderness of the Llanganati where he knew the Spanish would never attempt to go. Now, the spirit of Atahualpa watches over the treasure and curses anyone who comes to the Llanganati in search of it.'

"Carlos talked on, 'In the last 400 years, numerous deaths have occurred. The first to seek the gold was a Franciscan Monk named Father Longo who vanished into the night in 1535 while he sought the treasure at the request of King Charles V of Spain. The most recent was in 1960 when Mr. Holt, a geologist, led a treasure expedition into Llanganati. He died when he fell on a sharp broken tree stump that pierced his heart. Some say it was the ghost of Atahualpa who pushed him."

Barbara said, "Finish reading the transcript and you'll see how the indigenous peoples' belief in the curse played into Paulo's reluctance to say anything about my grandfather's disappearance."

I continued to read: *Diego did not find Mr. Green. When we got back to Quito, Diego kept his promise and paid our wages, and made me the guide for an archaeology expedition to an ancient Incan foundry. That exploration was successful, and Diego gave me his guide business, then returned to Spain.*

Before Dr. George hired me, I guided an expedition for a British botanist named Richard White, who sought Cinchona trees. At first, I refused to guide the expedition because the trees grow where Mr. Green vanished, but Mr. White offered me more money and said he had no interest in the Incan gold. I took the work and there were no problems. When Dr. George came along, he also wanted to go to the Cinchona tree area saying he had no interest in Incan gold. So, I agreed to guide him.

Dr. George had only four men, so I hired only two porters. The gringos were strong and sure-footed so we made Cinchona Valley in just forty-two days.

There were many Cinchona saplings since summer had just passed. We gathered the saplings, seeds, and bark and packed them in potato sacks. After two days of gathering, Dr. George had all he wanted. That night we sat by a warm fire and talked. Two of Dr. George's men started talking about the lost Inca treasure being close to us. I told them it was not good to talk about the treasure, it would only bring trouble. They laughed and kept talking. I got up and left, for fear something bad would happen.

That night Atahualpa came to me in a dream and said I should climb the mountain to the east in the morning. I obeyed him and climbed the mountain east above the jungle trees. By then, the sun had risen over the mountain and lit up the west mountain where the expedition was camped below. As I sat on a rock looking across the valley wondering why I was sent there, I saw two men climbing the west mountain. I could tell by their clothes they were the same two men that talked about the Incan treasure. I yelled for them to turn around and go back down the mountain, but they kept climbing. Stopping on a ledge, they moved some rocks that blocked a cave. I stood up, waving and yelling, but it did no good. They squeezed themselves through a small opening and came back out holding what looked like a golden sun disk. This provoked Atahualpa. The sky turned black. Lightning, thunder and a torrent of rain came down without wind. The earth started to move, and the whole side of the west mountain collapsed, burying them and the expedition below.

One moment, I was trying to see through darkness at what had befallen the men;the next moment the sun was shining in a clear blue sky. I could see the scar on the side of the west mountain. Fearful, I went back to the camp site to see what was under the mud, rocks, and trees. Everyone was dead.

I found Dr. George's body under a fallen tree. I removed him and buried him and his possessions in a clear part of the campsite next to a black rock slab that was the size of a coffin. Darkness was coming, and I had to start back to Spectacle Valley where I could get a horse and food.

As you know, Roberto, it is too dangerous to try to walk in the Llanganati at night. I found a place to sleep which was still in the valley of the Cinchona trees. I did not sleep well, but sometime in the night, whether I was asleep or awake, Atahualpa, came to me again. He said, he spared my life because I believed in him and the curse. I was to go back to my village where I would marry and have sons and would remain in his favor as long as I never spoke of having been a guide for expeditions into the Llanganati. I promised to abide by his wishes and have never broken my promise. Now, I have broken our bargain, as Pizarro did, but I will never tell where the treasure is hidden. Perhaps, Atahualpa will forgive me.

Barbara and I sat another half hour after I finished reading, discussing her intention to go to Ecuador to recover her grandfather's remains.

"Maybe tomorrow, when you have a chance, you can go to a secure phone and call Roberto," I suggested. "See if Paulo is willing to guide us. If not, I'm not optimistic your quest will succeed. After seventy-five years the burial site could be covered by dense jungle. We will need Paulo."

The next morning, she called Roberto from her office at the college and arranged a meeting with him and Paulo when we reached Ecuador. When she came home, I called Bob Berry at the police station from the house tapped phone

"Bob, I'm at Miss Anderson's house in Weston."

"So, that's where you are. I've been calling you all morning."

"It's 10:00 a.m. I'll be home in about an hour and will call you when I get in. I have access to some information the goons were looking for when they ran Henry off the road."

"I'll wait for your call," Bob said.

"What information will you give them?" Barbara asked before I left.

"Nothing I'm going to share. I just tossed some bait in the water over the tapped phone. They'll come calling, and I'll find out who they are. I know they want it."

"Be careful," she said. "Now, you're on their radar."

Chapter 10

E vents of the last twenty-four hours had my mind so occupied that I couldn't recall how I drove through traffic to get to the North End. I parked in my off-street parking space, and stepped out into a cold, sunny day. The walk to my apartment took me past Mr. Martinelli's store. He noticed me through his large window displaying fruit and vegetables, and signaled for me to wait. The Bentley was in a repair shop, so I didn't expect him to tell me that he'd seen it.

After he'd finished with his last customer, Mr. Martinelli came out into the freezing, crackling air and, as usual, was dressed only in a white dress shirt tucked into baggy pants. He stood on the sidewalk talking to me without a shiver.

Maybe he's a human solar pane, I thought, *since the sun is shining on him.*

"Anthony, I no see your Bentley."

"I found it! Thank you for watching."

"Anthony, you might have trouble."

"Why?"

"Come here and look around the corner."

I walked to the corner and Martinelli pointed to a black
Caddy parked halfway down the block.

"You see that black Cadillac?"

I nodded yes.

"Anthony, about half an hour ago, two men got out of that
car, walked right past my store, and went into your flat."

"What did they look like?"

"You have seen *Casablanca,* Anthony?"

"Yes, I have, several times."

"Thirty years ago, when I first saw the picture, I fall in
love with Ingrid Bergman. I still love her and watch the movie
many times."

"Well?"

"The picture, Anthony. One of the men is small and looks
like Peter Lorre. You know, the big eyes. The other man has a fat,
round face. Walks with a cane with silver trim. I not make-a joke,
he looks a little like Sydney Greenstreet."

A customer entered his store and Martinelli followed him
inside while warning me that the little guy was dangerous. I
thanked him and said, "Maybe I could arrange a meeting with
Ingrid and you."

"Bah! *Bona Fortuna.* "

I walked to the polished Cadillac, a boxy 1971 Eldorado.
The driver's side had some minor scratches. I memorized the
Massachusetts numbers on the license plate. Its registration tag
was good until July 1972, and the inspection sticker glued to the
windshield was also good though 1972. The doors were locked,
so I looked though the passenger window and saw the inside
was clean except for an open can of Planters peanuts on the
center console. Only minor scratches ruled it out as being the car

that slammed into Henry.

Mr. Martinelli was right, the two men who drove the Cadillac were in my flat.

I walked up three granite steps leading to the front door of my building and peered inside the dimly lit hallway. My apartment was straight ahead at the end of the hall, past a set of stairs that led to a second-floor apartment rented by two young working women. My apartment door was solid oak and fitted with a skeleton key lock. I turned doorknob. The door moved. It was unlocked. I hadn't left it that way.

Not sure what to expect, I unholstered my Glock and held it in my right hand as I gently pushed the door halfway open with my foot. It opens into my kitchen. The fat man was sitting on a kitchen chair facing the door. His black full-length overcoat and fedora hat were placed on another kitchen chair. He was bald and looked like a white Sumo wrestler dressed in a dark gray three-piece suit. His hands were below his chin resting on the silver top of his walking stick. The man's grey eyes revealed an intelligent, mild tempered man.

"Mr. April, you have arrived at last. Please come in, this is your home."

Even though both of his hands were on top of his walking stick, I remained in the hallway, remembering Mr. Martinelli's words, "Two men went into your apartment." The little guy wasn't making himself visible. I scanned the pantry, the parlor, my bedroom. The only place I couldn't see was the bathroom because the half open door blocked my view. I tried looking through the space between my apartment door and the door jam. Yep. There was Peter Lorre, with a silver gun in his hand, standing behind the door.

I quickly stepped into the room just far enough to ram the door into the wall with my shoulder. For a moment, I thought the heavy oak door would go right through the wall, but fortunately the little guy's body cushioned the door from damaging it. As I leaned against the door, there had been no pushback. Now, stepping away from the door, it slowly swung closed as Peter slid down the wall and rolled against the door frame. He was out like a light, blood flowing down his chin onto his ski jacket sleeve, then onto my wooden oak floor. His nose was flattened. It hadn't looked too big to begin with. Even so, he was now in a dark world, but still clutched a 7.65 Beretta m9 in his right hand. I took the gun and sat him up so the blood would run on him and not on my floor.

"Mr. April there was no need for such violence. Look what you have done to poor Rocco."

'Sorry, but I don't like playing peekaboo with guns."

So, the little guy's first name was Rocco, not Peter.

"Rocco was only there to protect me in case you became aggressive."

As we spoke, I got a good look at him. He was definitely a heavyweight, maybe three hundred pounds plus. Though sitting down, I guessed him to be less than six feet tall. He appeared to be in his late fifties, nattily dressed, peering at me with gray eyes that portrayed a man who made the road he walked down.

"Mr. April, please attend to poor Rocco. His blood will get all over his clothes."

Rocco could continue to bleed as far as I was concerned, but I didn't want the blood on my floor. I went to the bathroom, got a couple of towels. soaked one with water and cleaned Rocco's bloodied face. As I cleaned him, he came to. It took a few minutes for him to understand what had happened before he jerked the towels out of my hands and nursed his broken nose. His Peter Lorre thyroid eyes were half shut; he wasn't in any shape or disposition to give me trouble.

"Now, that Rocco is taken care of, you can fill me in as to why you are here, Mr…"

"Rhodes. Sydney Rhodes, not Dusty Rhodes, please." At least Sydney had a sense of humor and was direct in saying what he wanted.

"Mr. April, I'm here to offer you a sizable amount of money for the map to the lost Inca treasure, I believe you have in your possession."

"A map to lost Incan treasure? I don't have a treasure map."

"Not 'a' map. The map used during Dr. Anderson's expedition."

Obviously, he wasn't talking about the map in *National Geographic.*

Old Sydney read my blank expression.

"I thought you had the map in your possession, but it appears you do not. Well, no matter, I believe you will acquire it soon, and when you do, we can come to an agreement on the sum of money I will pay you for it."

If there was such a map, I had no intention of making a deal with Sydney for it, but I played along.

"How do I contact you when I have the map?"

He took his right hand off the top of his cane and reached into his jacket side pocket. I felt my body tense. Then, as I watched his hand came out of his pocket with a calling card, I relaxed.

"You're a cautious man, Mr. April. Here is my business card. Call the Boston number."

The card also listed a Nassau, Bahamas phone number for 'Antiquities, Ltd'.

"After I let you know I have the map, what assurance do I have that you and Rocco won't be here again to take it from me or run me off the road, like you did Miss Anderson's chauffeur?"

"Mr. April, I have an intense dislike for violence. I came here to offer money, not to rob you. I can assure you that neither Rocco nor I had anything to do with Miss Anderson's chauffeur being pushed off the road."

"But you know about it," I said.

"Yes, I know about it."

Somehow, he had access to info from Barbara's tapped phone, but I didn't want him to know that I knew, so dropped the subject. The meeting with Sydney didn't make sense. I still believed Wilson tapped Barbara's phone to know what she was doing to find Dr. Anderson's burial site, and possibly his diary. It wouldn't be until much later in Ecuador when the puzzle pieces would finally come together

The visit was over. Sydney struggled as he rose from the chair using his cane to pry himself up. In his way, Sydney had conveyed that he had access to both past and future information which he wasn't going to reveal. He looked over at Rocco, who was now standing by the door, nursing his broken nose.

"Rocco it's time for us to leave, and get you to a doctor. I am asking Mr. April to give you back your pistol. We do not want to harm him. Isn't that correct Rocco?"

Rocco nodded in the affirmative, though his eyes said something entirely different.

I removed the rounds and handed him the Beretta. The oaken door had changed his facial features—now he looked more like Jake La Motta after his fight with Sugar Ray Robinson at the Chicago Stadium. Both eyes were almost closed and were starting to turn black and blue. When Rocco took the gun, he pointed the muzzle at my head.

I got his message loud and clear. I had made a deadly enemy and answered his threat with a contemptuous smile. As he put the gun in his coat pocket, I noted that his one visible eye questioned my smile. He kept it on me until he walked out the door with Sydney. Rocco would prove to be one tough little bastard.

Chapter 11

I met Bob at Nico's Restaurant on Hanover Street a little after noon. When I walked in, he was already seated at a table by a window. He had a view of parked cars and tourists ambling by, bundled tightly against the clear, frigid air. Sunlight streamed in from the window brightening a mural of the Roman Colosseum on a wall behind him.

I could tell from his ruddy Irish face that he had just come in from the cold. He peered at me, expressionless.

"You look out of place in here, Irish," I said.

"Sit down, Wop, and maybe they'll serve us. I have to leave in a little over half an hour."

We each ordered a meatball sandwich and a beer. Then, I brought him up to speed beginning with my driving Barbara from Logan to Weston last night and ending with my conversation with her this morning. Bob smiled knowingly, when I told him I'd spent the night at her house, but I ignored the insinuation. As I started to tell him about what Mr. Martinelli had said this morning, Angelo brought lunch and our conversation halted abruptly.

The tantalizing aroma of the foot-long loaf of fresh Italian bread sliced through the middle, stuffed with meatballs and covered with earthy tomato sauce, made my mouth water. We both attacked the food, and between mouthfuls, I listened as Bob provided his thoughts on whether the Bruins would make the Stanley Cup playoffs.

In ten minutes, the food and beer had evaporated. Jenny, Angelo's pretty and busty bleached blonde waitress, sashayed over to our table. She leaned over to clean the table flaunting rounded twin peaks above her low-cut dress.

Bob pointed to a spot on the table in front of him: "Here's a spill, Jenny."

She smiled, deliberately taking her time to clean the imaginary spot. As she wiped, she looked up at Bob and drawled, "Anything else you'd like?"

"I'll have two of those," Bob said. After a beat, he pointed to the Miller beer bottles.

Jenny laughed, enjoying her flirtation, then got our beers.

After Bob assured me that his mind was clear, I continued my story about the morning's events. I told him how Mr. Martinelli had warned: "Anthony, two men went into your building and didn't come out," and detailed my encounter with Sydney and Rocco.

Bob's first comment, after I finished was: "You should've shot Rocco for breaking and entering. He was armed. Someday you'll regret you didn't."

I picked my beer glass off the table which left a wet circle that I smeared out with my fingers.

"Maybe, but there was enough of his blood on my floor; I didn't need any more. Besides, I need Sydney to believe I'm working with him in order to find out why he thinks the Inca treasure map exists. If there is a map, Paulo would have it."

"Who's Paulo?"

I told him the secret that I had sworn to keep, having full trust in Bob.

"Roberto's father, Paulo, the expedition's guide, is still alive." Then, proceeded to tell the backstory that Paulo had told his son.

"After hearing this, I agree that Paulo would be the only one who might have a map to the treasure," said Bob, "but fearing Atahualpa's curse, I doubt he would keep it. Still, after Roberto talked to him, he might've drawn a map pinpointing where Dr. Anderson is buried."

"If someone knew how Dr. Anderson died, they could use that map to locate the treasure," I said.

"There are only four people who can link the Inca treasure to where Dr. Anderson is buried—Paulo, Roberto, Barbara, and you," Bob noted. "Am I missing anyone?"

"It appears Sydney and the NSA have made the connection too," I replied.

"You think they could've learned it from the tapped phones of Roberto and Barbara's conversations?"

"Possibly. I'm going to Ecuador and set up an expedition to recover Dr. Anderson's remains. I'll be working with Paulo and Roberto. They might own up to whether a map exists, and if it does, how someone would have learned about it."

Bob didn't comment, just pushed back from the table saying he had to leave, and asked me to keep him posted. His chair legs screeched so loudly on the tile floor that other diners near us turned to look. Oblivious to the disturbance he'd made, he threw a ten on the table, more than enough to cover his meal and tip. I watched him walk out the door into the cold sunshine and said to myself: *You don't know it yet, Bobby, but you're going on the expedition.*

I paid the tab and walked to the Boston Public Library on Boylston Street. There was a deep desire to learn more about the sinking of the battleship *Maine,* and why it led to the Spanish American war. I started with the 1897 editions of *The Boston Globe,* and the *Boston Herald* on microfilm. The papers mainly quoted articles about Cuban atrocities committed by Spain and published in William Randolph Hearst's *New York World,* and Joseph Pulitzer's *New York Journal.* The reports of rape, torture, and inhumane treatment of Cubans I was reading had subsequently been found to be widely distorted or fabricated. The relentless "yellow journalism" promoted the call for Cuban intervention.

President McKinley did *not* want to go to war with Spain. The military, led by Under Secretary of the Navy, Theodore Roosevelt, *wanted* war with Spain in order to relieve the United States of European domination, and advance its security in the Pacific and the Caribbean. McKinley was working on an agreement with Spain to turn Cuba over to its people. The press set upon him as a weak, naive President, and banged the war drum daily, pressuring him to authorize war with Spain. A significant event was needed to persuade him, and the destruction of the *Maine* in Havana Harbor, Cuba, on February 15, 1898, provided that event.

On March 21, 1898, the Board of Inquiry led by Captain Sampson, concluded that the *Maine* was destroyed by a mine. The Board discounted testimony that a likely cause was a bunker located next to the magazine stores filled with bituminous coal. The coal had created firedamp gas, which was prone to spontaneous explosion. But the Board concluded there were no accelerants in the area to ignite the gas.

Additional sighted evidence and testimony given by both Spanish and United States weapons experts, were consistent with an internal explosion. A mine exploding underwater would have raised a column of water and killed fish. Yet no geyser of water had been seen, and there were no dead fish. The weapons specialist testified that a ship's ammunition stores would never be detonated by a mine. The board still concluded a Spanish mine was to blame.

Even though Pulitzer privately felt that "nobody outside a lunatic asylum" believed Spain had sunk the *Maine*, the *Journal* and *World* continued to drive the American public to a frenzy. "Remember the Maine" and "To Hell with Spain" were written in articles daily. McKinley finally yielded, and on April 20, 1898, Congress adopted a resolution declaring war against Spain.

After researching for over two hours, I got up to stretch my legs and drift around the room filled with desks and microfilm machines. Only one other person was in the room, a young blonde girl wearing a red Boston College Eagles cap, and reading microfilm.

When my ten-minute break was over, I read the 1911 Vreeland Board inquiry into the sinking which agreed with the 1898 Sampson Board finding that the *Maine* was destroyed by a Spanish mine. It dismissed the theory that the sinking was caused by exploding bituminous coal gas because they also concluded there were no accelerants present in the coal bunker that could have caused the explosion.

I sat back in my chair recalling what Dr. George Anderson had written to his wife about what he saw on his tour of the

Maine: A fellow visitor had looked through the inspection port and dropped a cigar-shaped object into the coal bunker.

Was it a delayed accelerant device used to ignite the gas? I now wondered. Did he mean to create the explosion, destroy the Maine, and create a false flag? Did history get it wrong... on purpose?

Chapter 12

Before I left the library, I made my first entries of the Anderson case in a pocket notebook:

Anderson Case

10 March 1972

Tasks:

- Call Barbara at 7 p.m.
- Ask if she's heard of or talked about a map of Dr. A's expedition
- Go over her telephone conversations with Roberto again
- Any arrangements on trip to Ecuador?
- Does she know Sydney or Rocco?
- Talk to Henry about how hard the cars hit

Facts:

- Paulo Sanchez, the expedition guide, is alive
- He knows where Dr. Anderson is buried and the location of the Inca treasure
- Paulo buried the Doc.'s possessions with him

- Sydney wants the Inca treasure
- Wilson wants the diary
- Barbara wants her grandfather's remains
- Paulo wants everyone to go away
- The Rickover Committee is questioning Barbara
- Cuba and Spain are still saying the sinking was a False Flag

Assumptions:
- Wilson tapped Barbara's phone
- Sydney has access to the tapped phone
- The diary contains the name of the man who may have caused *Maine* to sink
- NSA wants control of diary or to destroy it—has failed to identify past false flags
- Wilson won't remain in background much longer

I put the notebook in my coat, removed the microfilm from its viewer, and shut it off. The girl in the red Boston College cap was still the only other person in the room and deeply absorbed in reading microfilm and taking notes. Gathering my belongings, I left the room and returned the microfilm at the front desk. I, also, checked out two books: *The Sinking of the Battleship Maine*, and *Inca Gold: The Treasure of the Llanganatis.*

It was 5:15 p.m. when I left the library; the sun had set. Large, illuminated snowflakes were floating down past street-lamps and clinging to people's hats and coats. There was a pleasant rhythm to everything: the snow, the pedestrians, the slow-moving traffic. People were walking, going somewhere, for many reasons. My somewhere would soon be Ecuador, and my reason was to recover a dead man.

When I reached my apartment at 6:00 p.m., an inch of wet snow had accumulated on the three granite steps leading into the apartment building. The girls upstairs usually got home by six-thirty, so the absence of footprints gave me confidence I had no unwanted visitors.

In keeping with my limited culinary skills, I ate ziti *al dente* dunked in canned tomato sauce with two-day-old Italian bread, and a glass of Pisano red wine. While eating, I mused on the saying: "The way to a man's heart is through his stomach"

Ellen had been a good cook in addition to all her other loving qualities. Our relationship was over, and I couldn't fault her. We'd been going together for two years and she had wanted to get married. I didn't. The case was closed, and I would never hear from her again.

Now anxious to read the Inca treasure book from the library, I wanted to gain insight into the Incan's belief that anyone seeking the treasure would be cursed to die, and also learn of any maps made by treasure explorers. Leaving dirty dishes in the sink, I went to my exercise room and sat at my small, two-drawer wooden desk which held a lamp and pictures of my family along with a few of Ellen and me.

I knew most of the background about how the treasure came into being, so I read the details of how, why, and where it was said to be hidden:

> The Spanish Conquistador, Francisco Pizarro, made a bargain with the Incan Emperor, Atahualpa, whom he had imprisoned. Atahualpa said he would fill his prison cell with gold if Pizarro would set him free, and Pizarro agreed. For three months, gold and silver streamed in

from all corners of the Empire by way of peasants' backs. What Pizarro didn't know was that a caravan of 60,000 men under General Ruminahui with 750 tons of worked gold was on its way to Cajamarca. Unaware. Pizarro broke the bargain on August 29, 1533, when he garroted and burned Atahualpa at the stake. Rumjnahui, still enroute, learned of Atahualpa's murder, the incensed general hid the caravan of treasure in the dangerous Ecuadorian Llanganti mountains where the Spanish would never dare to go.

Sitting back, I mulled over what I'd learned: the size of the treasure was vast and hidden in the most dangerous mountains of the Llangantes.

I stretched while Mr. Coffee was brewing. When it finished, I took a cup of black coffee to my desk and read about past expeditions which had sought the treasure.

The first expedition was formed at the order of King Charles V of Spain, several decades after the death of Atahualpa, based on a written path to the treasure given to him by a Spanish adventurer, Valverde, who was married to an Incan queen. The leader of the expedition, a Franciscan monk named Father Longo, mysteriously vanished during the night when he believed the treasure was close.

Then, for over a hundred years the search for the treasure was abandoned until 1740. A man named Don Guzman, who worked in an old Llangantes mine, made a detailed map from Valverde's written path to the treasure. When his map indicated he was approaching the location of the hidden treasure, Guzman also disappeared during the night.

A hundred and twenty years later, in 1860, a British botanist doing research in the archives at Latacunga, Ecuador, stumbled upon the Guzman map. In 1866, he provided the map to two Nova Scotian treasure hunters, Captain Barth Blake and George Chapman, who formed an expedition and claimed success in finding the treasure. Blake, however, died in the mountains and Chapman died while sailing home. He fell overboard while holding an Incan gold sun disk and disappeared under the sea.

Having found a reference to the treasure map, I entered a note into my notebook: *Have Barbara ask Roberto to go to Latacunga archives for a copy of the Guzman map.* Then, went back to reading.

The 1920 expedition was formed by American banker, Colonel Brooks, who took along his wife for a romantic getaway. She died of pneumonia and he was locked up in a New York insane asylum for the rest of his life.

In the 1930 expedition, it rained 37 out of 39 days, and the porters accompanying Scotsman Erskine Loch, deserted him. Lacking food, he hallucinated and shot himself.

The 1960 expedition ended when gold miner Bob Holt, who financed the expedition, fell on a sharpened tree trunk which stabbed him directly in the heart.

After reading that no expedition looking for Atahualpa's hidden treasure had been exempt from tragedy, I understood the reason for Paulo's obsessive belief in the Atahualpa curse. Still, I wasn't a total believer until the curse struck during Barbara's planned 1972 expedition to find her grandfather's remains.

At 7:00 p.m., I called Barbara from my desk phone and Gretchen answered, saying that Barbara had just gotten home from work and was in the shower.

"I will let Miss Anderson know that you're on the phone. In the meantime, Henry would like to talk with you."

"Hello, Mr. April. How are you?"

"I'm fine. How are you feeling?"

"I'm feeling much better. But, I'm curious to know if you've learned anything about the men that forced me off the road."

"Nothing yet. But Detective Bob Berry, the fellow who was with me at the hospital, will let me know when the police have something, and I'll call you."

"Thanks."

"I do have a question for you, Henry. I assume the car that forced you into the abutment would have sustained some damage. What do you think?" I asked.

"This afternoon I went to the repair garage. The Bentley's passenger front door and fender are banged up. Part of a decal, which had to have been on their bumper, is embedded in the Bentley's fender, so I would think their car was damaged."

"Is any part of the decal readable?"

"To me, it looks like a piece of a blue and white sticker with a couple of smudged numbers, or letters, which I couldn't read."

"Henry, I would like you to call the repair shop, and ask them to hold off fixing the car for a couple of days. Bob and I will go down to take a look. Where is the car?"

"It's at Boston Bentley in Wayland." They both heard a click on the line.

"Bye, for now, Miss Anderson has picked up the phone."

"Sorry to keep you waiting," Barbara said. "How'd your day go?"

"I've had better. How was yours?"

"Good. Made some progress on our research project."

"Oh, I didn't know you were working on a research project."

"I'll tell you about it the next time we get together. It doesn't sound like your day went so well."

"It wasn't terrible, I've had worse. But, there are some things we have to talk about soon. When can we get together?" I didn't want to talk over the tapped phone. Besides, I wanted to see her, again.

"Tomorrow night around six would be good for me."

"How about me taking you to dinner?"

"Thank you, Tony, that's a nice offer, but I think it would be better to talk here. Gretchen can cook. She likes cooking for you. In fact, if I were you, I would be prepared to stay all night. Your room is available."

"I'm okay with staying. See you at six. Goodnight, Barbara."

"Goodnight, Tony."

I couldn't believe how much her voice had triggered a desire to be with her. Six o'clock tomorrow night seemed a long way off.

Funny, I'd thought those emotions were over for me.

How could I know that within 24 hours, those emotions would turn from love to hate.

Chapter 13

At 6:15 a.m., I awoke feeling it was going to be a good day. Looking out the parlor window, I checked the weather and fired up the coffee pot. The sun was still below the three-story apartment building across the street, yet light had already begun to wash away the dark. Two pedestrians were plodding along on the sidewalk; coat collars turned up to shelter faces from the wind driven snow. I tuned in to a Boston radio station for the day's weather forecast.

"Temperature in our area is currently 26 degrees Fahrenheit with an expected high of 30 degrees later today," the forecaster was saying.

The coffee brewed as I entered tasks for the day in my notebook:

15 March 1972

- *Call Bob. See if he can go to Wayland today and check the Bentley*
- *Weston for dinner at six. Pick up a bottle of wine*

- *Go over notes with Barbara*

After finishing my coffee, I prepared for a five-mile run. Donning gym shorts, a white long-sleeved tee shirt, black Adidas fleece sweatshirt and pants, Converse running shoes, a Bruins sock cap, and black ski gloves, I was bundled and hit the street. Three blocks from the end of my run, I stopped at a pier of an abandoned fish processing plant.

When I was younger, I came to the pier often to watch fishermen unload their catches. The boats were tied to the pier which circled the plant. Wooden ladders, used by fishermen to climb up and down from their boats, extended from the top of the pier to the harbor bed and were spaced about fifty feet apart.

Baskets of fish were pulleyed up and dumped onto a conveyor that passed in front of a dozen women armed with their own sharpened filet knives. If you wanted to see how they filleted a fish, you didn't blink. Once passed the women, a conveyor belt carried the fillets along for processing while the remainder of carcasses were thrown to another conveyor dumping into a grinder.

The mash was then pumped into the hold of another boat for transport to animal food manufacturers. I remembered the stink of fish parts was so bad I had to breathe through my mouth to keep from gagging. Today, the memory of fish stench was replaced with a pleasant aroma of fresh ocean air.

By now, the sun was well above the horizon. I didn't know why, but the sight of the historic black and white trimmed *USS Constitution* docked in Charlestown brought me loving thoughts of Barbara. Unfortunately, it didn't last long. Curious about the tide level, I leaned over between ladder posts to check things.

One ladder's highwater mark was now about eight feet above the water which meant it was low tide or close to it. As I stared at the polluted brown water twenty feet below, Rocco, hidden by a corner of the building ten feet away, snuck up and launched me off the pier.

"Have a good swim, April!"

The twenty-foot fall took just over a second but, instinctively, my military cold-water submersion training kicked in.

Get your feet under you in case you hit bottom or an obstruction. I figured I was about five feet out from the ladder.

Hold your breath. Fight the gasp reflex so you don't swallow water. When I entered the liquid below, my sweats and gloves prevented instant contact with icy water from shocking the bulk of my body. I expected the head pain, and pressed my lips together hard, willing my mouth to stay closed so I wouldn't gasp for breath. Dying in combat would be ok, but drowning would not.

The cuffs of my sweatpants trapped air and prevented a deep descent, so I didn't strike bottom or any obstruction, but that was the end of the good news. I tried opening my eyes, but found only complete darkness because any surface light was obscured by polluted water.

As I fell, I heard the roar of water in my ears; now there was complete silence. The weight of my saturated sweat clothes pulled me toward the bottom. I kicked hard against the firm surface, while pulling my hands down to my sides from above my head.

But without visible surface light to orient myself, I couldn't tell if I was going up, down or sideways. Then I began to make out brown surface light which kept growing brighter. The next second I broke the surface, sucking in great lungsful of frigid air. I was ten feet from a ladder. The tide was slack, and despite the weight of the waterlogged clothes and shoes, I made it to the ladder. My hat was gone.

As I pulled myself out of the water, I inhaled another deep breath and looked up to see Rocco's bandaged face peering down at me.

"How's the water April? Nice day for a swim." He continued to taunt me. "You're lucky the boss wants you alive or I would have put a bullet in you."

Well, that was comforting.

By the time I climbed to the top, Rocco was gone. I quickly removed my shoes and socks, and stripped off my sodden clothes, only keeping my gym shorts on. Then, threw everything against the building.

Ice was starting to form on my hair and eyebrows, as I shivered with mild hypothermia. Putting my wet shoes back on, I ran for home, not caring about people who stopped and stared at the nearly naked man with frosted hair running past them.

Some yellow hard hat workers watched me running, then yelled: "Hey, Romeo, did your girlfriend's husband come home?" I ran on, ignoring catcalls like "Nut Cake."

When I finally reached my building, I shivered while taking my key out of soaked shorts. Then with hands shaking badly, I had to steady my right hand with my left, just to find the keyhole. Two steps in, I shed my shoes and shorts, and stripped a blanket off my bed to cover myself.

Still dripping as I headed for the bathroom, I nearly slipped on the bare oak floors. Then, reaching for a bath towel, I yanked it off its rack and wiped away the ice crystals clinging to my hair and eyebrows. Knowing better than to shower, I realized hot water would direct blood to my skin and could cause low blood pressure, organ failure, and possibly death. It was good to know these things beforehand rather than find out later.

Finally, wrapped in the blanket, I walked around for twenty minutes until the shivering stopped and my body temperature began to recover. I put on the coffee pot and took a warm shower, scrubbing the polluted water from every inch of my body.

I dried off, gargled with hydrogen peroxide, and put on lotion and deodorant. Then I dressed, gathered up my gym shorts, towels, and blanket for the laundry, and threw out my running shoes.

Refreshed, I sat at the kitchen table, drank coffee and fantasized about throwing that little bastard, Rocco, into Boston Harbor and watching him drown.

After a while, when I had finished a couple more cups of coffee and drowned Rocco a few more times in my imagination, I called Bob and asked him to come with me to check the mark on the Bentley. He said he'd be available at two o'clock, and to pick him up at the police station. I didn't mention my morning swim.

At the dealership we were met by Pamela, an attractive middle-aged blonde receptionist wearing a pearl necklace and earrings to make rich buyers feel they had come to the right place. We asked for Thomas White, the dealership manager, and she paged him. We rejected her offer of refreshments, and walked over to inspect a black mirror-polished T1 Bentley floor model while we waited.

"Just your style," Bob said.

"Hey, maybe someday I'll buy one and hire you to drive me around."

"How can I help you gentlemen?" asked a voice from behind us.

By the tone of his voice, he'd either overheard our conversation or had sized-up our net worth. We turned around and faced Thomas White who appeared to be in his forties with a full head of well-groomed light brown hair, dark blue eyes, and rounded face. He was dressed in a dark blue two-piece suit over a lighter blue turtleneck.

"I'm Detective Bob Berry with the Boston Police, and this is Tony April, private investigator," Bob said. "We're here to examine Miss Anderson's damaged Bentley."

"Yes, I did get a call from Miss Anderson's chauffeur not to start repairs until you inspected it. A Mr. Roger Brown from the insurance company was also here this morning to assess the damage."

White reached into his jacket pocket. "If you need to talk to him, here's his business card."

Bob took the card, putting it into his top coat pocket. "Thanks, we may just do that."

"The Bentley is parked in back. You won't miss it; it's the only damaged one out there. The doors aren't locked. Do you need any assistance?"

"No, we'll manage," Bob said. "If we have any questions, we'll ask before we leave."

We found the car behind the building, backed up to a security fence. There were two inches of fresh snow on the ground and the car's roof. The main damage was easily seen on the driver's side: left front end tilted down, driven into the blown tire. Glass was broken on both the left headlight and signal light.

We turned to each other with the same thought: Something's

wrong here.

"You see what I see?" Bob asked.

"The snow."

"Yeah, the snow. We had a couple of inches of new snow last night, and..."

"No footprints," I cut in. "The snow is untouched on this side. An adjuster would have trekked all around it to assess the damage. Somebody's lying."

There were tracks on the passenger side of the Bentley. They ended in a section of trampled snow by the wheel well where Henry had described the location of an embedded bumper sticker. Closer inspection showed the sticker had been scraped off, probably into a container because the snow below the scrapes was clean. With all the trampled snow, we noted one clean print visible.

"Look there; that's an unusual shoe pattern," Bob took the insurance card out of his pocket and drew a likeness on the back.

"Let's go inside and make a call."

Pamela allowed us to use the phone, and Bob dialed the number for Atlas Insurance Company listed on Roger Brown's business card. A woman answered.

"Good afternoon. Atlas Insurance. This is Rita."

"Roger Brown, please," Bob said.

"Mr. Brown no longer works here. He retired three years ago. Can another agent help you?"

"He retired three years ago?"

"Yes, he worked as an adjuster for Atlas for thirty-five years and has moved to Florida. Were you a client of his?"

"No, I found his Atlas Insurance business card."

"The only thing he's adjusting these days is his anchor line on his fishing boat," Rita said.

"Thanks for the update," Bob said and hung up the phone. "As we expected, whoever removed the remnants of the decal, wasn't an insurance agent.".

I had Pamela page Mr. White, and we met on the showroom floor.

"Did you find Miss Anderson's car?"

"Yes, we did," I said.

"Well, then, how can I help you?"

"Can you please describe Mr. Brown?" I asked.

"No, I can't because I never met him. I was in our morning sales meeting. Pamela brought in his business card and told me what he wanted. I asked her to tell him where Miss Anderson's car was parked, and if he had any questions, I would be out of my meeting in approximately half an hour. He left before the meeting ended, so I never met him. I am sure Pamela can help you."

White walked us over to Pamela.

"Mr. Berry and Mr. April have some questions about the Atlas insurance man. Please help them. I'll be in my office."

"Pamela, what time did Mr. Brown arrive? Bob asked.

"We open at eight-thirty. When I unlocked the door this morning, he was standing outside waiting to get in."

"Then, you didn't see him drive up?" Bob asked.

"No, I didn't."

"What did he say when you let him in?"

"He said he was Roger Brown from Atlas Insurance Company and that he needed to appraise the damage to Miss Anderson's Bentley. He went on to say that he just needed to know where the car was stored, and didn't need any help examining the damage. I told him I still had to inform Mr. White, our dealership manager. However, Mr. White was in a morning sales meeting and didn't like to be interrupted.

"That's when he handed me his business card and said he had to go to another appointment. Could I just give Mr. White his card and get his OK to check the car, he would greatly appreciate it. He repeated that he didn't need any help."

"Then you gave the card to Mr. White, and he gave permission for Brown to see the car?" I asked.

"Yes."

"Would you please describe Mr. Brown to us?" Bob asked.

"He was tall, maybe six feet or a little more, clean shaven, blue eyes and blonde hair. He was an attractive man, probably in his thirties."

"How was he dressed?"

"He was wearing a black felt fedora hat and a black, military style wool topcoat with navy blue pants. Oh, yes, he wore black leather gloves, and black galoshes. The best dressed adjuster I've ever seen."

"You didn't see the car he was driving?" Bob asked.

"No, I didn't see him drive in or out. He mustn't have been here long. By the time I got to my desk after making the coffee and setting out snacks out for our customers, he'd left."

"Did Mr. Brown ever remove his gloves?" Bob asked.

"No. As a matter of fact, I was curious as to why he kept his gloves on when taking his business card out of his wallet. It would have been less difficult had he removed his gloves. Is Mr. Brown in trouble?"

"No, we're just looking into circumstances of the Bentley accident. Thanks for your help, Pamela, you've been great," Bob said as we left.

We drove back to the car and drove back to the North End.

"What did you learn from this trip?" Bob asked.

"The decal smudge was removed so it couldn't be used to lead us to the men who ran Henry off the road."

"How'd Brown's impersonator know part of a decal was on the Bentley?"

"Because Henry told him," I replied.

"*Henry* told him?"

"Yes, but not directly. He told me about the decal over Barbara's tapped phone. The big surprise is how close Pamela's description of Mr. Brown fits Chuck Wilson."

Chapter 14

At exactly 6:00 p.m., I entered Barbara's moonlit snow-covered driveway. My headlights lit up a black sedan with a white Maryland license plate parked by the front door. I wasn't happy to see it.

Damn, wanted to spend this entire evening alone with Barbara, I thought, grabbing the bottle of wine as I slammed the car door. One set of footprints led from the sedan to the house. I recognized the same size and sole pattern as those at the Bentley dealership. Bending over, I was getting a closer look, when Henry came out without a jacket or hat, holding a lightbulb.

"Mr. April, did you drop something?"

"No, I was just curious if these footprints were made by a man or a woman."

"They were made by a man. He's in the library with Miss Barbara."

"Do you know him?"

"Never saw him before. I heard the doorbell ring when I was in the foyer closet looking for a lightbulb. Gretchen answered the door before I could. They talked for a moment, the man stepped inside, and Gretchen took him to the library."

"Was he wearing a black felt hat and black military-style coat?"

"I'm impressed! You saw all that in his footprint?"

"I'll show you how to do it later. Right now, I want to check on Miss Barbara."

Henry rang the doorbell for me and left to change a burnt out bulb. I stomped the snow off my shoes on the welcome mat and waited.

Gretchen opened the door. "Good evening, Mr. April."

"Good evening, Gretchen."

"Miss Barbara is in the library with a Colonel Wilson. I'll take your hat and coat. Miss Barbara said that when you arrived, I should not bring you into the library; she would come out."

I handed Gretchen the bottle of red chianti classic reserve wine along with my hat and coat. She hung my hat and coat in the foyer closet, set the wine by the Tiffany lamp on a small table and went to the library. While I waited for Barbara, I checked my watch against the foyer Grandfather clock. They agreed to the minute: 6:17.

I wondered why Wilson would come to see Barbara after scraping off the decal. Maybe there was nothing to it.

"Mr. April, Miss Barbara is coming out."

"Thank you, Gretchen," I said as she strode off to the kitchen with the wine, her posture straighter than a general's. When Barbara came out of the library, I didn't move, captivated by her beauty. We met in the middle of the foyer, and she clasped both my hands with her warm, soft ones.

"Tony, only two days have passed since we were together, but it seems so much longer."

"I feel the same way."

"Hopefully, Colonel Wilson won't stay too long. I haven't invited him to dinner."

"Did he just show up at the door?"

"No, he called about an hour ago from Boston. He said he was driving by Weston on his way to D.C. and would like to meet and talk about my intention to retrieve Grandfather's remains."

"Did he say what he was doing in Boston?"

"No."

"We'd better go in. Be careful, he'll pump us for information that can lead to things we don't want him to know, like Paulo being alive," she said in a low voice.

I didn't want Barbara to know about Wilson's trip to the Bentley dealership before she went back in. If anyone was going to mention it, I wanted it to be Wilson.

As we entered the library, Chuck rose from the sofa and firmly shook my hand. He hadn't changed much in the five years since we'd bummed around together in Panama. His blonde hair had grayed some, and his dark Panama tan was gone, but he was still in good physical shape. His dapper dress style hadn't changed. He wore a navy-blue blazer, navy blue pants, and a light blue shirt, with no tie.

"Thank you for recommending me to Miss Anderson," I said.

"I recommended you because Miss Anderson insists on going to the Llanganati, and I know of no one better than you, to accompany her on such a dangerous journey."

Barbara interrupted, "Why don't we sit down by the fire. I'll have Gretchen bring in drinks. What would you like, Colonel Wilson?"

"Water, please. I'll be driving to Washington when I leave and prefer not to drink any alcohol."

We all agreed to have water. Gretchen brought in a silver tray holding a Waterford pitcher full of water, three glasses, and a silver bucket of ice. Placing everything on the coffee table in front of us, she put four ice cubes in each glass, poured the water over them, then left the room.

Barbara and I sat in high-backed tan leather armchairs facing Wilson on the sofa. We were all sideways to the wood burning fireplace. For a few moments, we sipped our water and were drawn to introspection by the flicker of flames. It was peaceful. Then Barbara broke our silence.

"What brought you to Boston, Colonel?"

"I came to Boston for several reasons, all of them related to Admiral Rickover's inquiry into the sinking of the *Maine.* The National Security Agency is under pressure to provide his committee with intelligence on the sinking. Your grandfather's diary is a critical part to the investigation. We have information that you have in your possession a map used during the expedition and are withholding it from the committee."

"Where did you get that information? If I had such a map I would've told you. I simply want to recover my grandfather's remains."

"Some speculate that the map's substantial value is your motivation for keeping it."

"What makes anyone believe the expedition map is valuable?" Barbara asked.

"Your grandfather, in his research to find the location of Cinchona trees, obtained a 1500-year old map which was given to Father Longo, a Franciscan monk, by King Charles V of Spain, to recover the lost treasure of the Inca. When Father Longo disappeared in the mountains, his Inca Indian guide took the map. It remained hidden until your grandfather acquired it from his guide who gave him the map to locate the Cinchona tree valley, not the lost treasure of the Inca. Today there are hunters of the treasure that would pay thousands of dollars and a share of the treasure for the map."

"I assure you, Colonel, I have no interest in the treasure at all. So, what makes you think I have the map?"

Wilson leaned forward in his chair. "Do you recall the name Johnathan Barns?"

"Yes, I do. He was the ten-year-old cabin boy aboard the *Adventurer.*"

"After you sent me your grandfather's letter, I looked into the possibility that a member of the expedition who remained on the boat while it was being repaired, was still alive. Well, that is the same Johnathan Barns who lives and breathes in the Navy Retirement Home in the North End. At eighty-three years of age, his recall of the expedition events is excellent. Allow me to read his statement."

"Please do," Barbara said.

I was in Captain McGee's quarters when he and Dr. Anderson were looking at a map spread out on the Captain's desk. Dr. Anderson told how he had gotten the map from his Inca guide. It was a 16th century map that would lead to the lost treasure of the Inca which is said to be in the valley of the Cinchona trees. He'd convinced his guide that he was solely interested in the Cinchona tree valley, so the guide allowed him to make a copy of the map after the guide eliminated the precise location of the Inca treasure.

"I asked Barns, if he knew what happened to the map."

When the doctor didn't return from the expedition, we sailed back to Boston. Captain McGee instructed me to put the Professor's belongings in his sea chest. I put the map, some books, letters and few items of clothing into the chest. Captain McGee returned it to the doctor's wife.

"So, you see why I believe you have the map,"

"I've never seen a chest that belonged to my grandfather."

"I believe you, but I'll bet the chest is somewhere on this property."

I watched Barbara's expression go from incredulous to contemplative. His belief that Barbara had the map shed some light on why he had tapped her phone, and why Sydney believed I could get it.

What remained unanswered was Sydney's access to the tapped phone conversations and why Wilson scraped the remains of an emblem off the Bentley. I wanted to ask but held off. Instead, I rose and put a log on the fire. When I sat down, again, I looked at Barbara.

"Do you think it's possible that your grandfather's sea chest is here?"

"I suppose it's possible," she said. "This house has a large attic which has accumulated stuff for over a 150 years. Once, as a child, I peeked through the trap door into the attic, but ever since, have had no desire to go into its musty, hidden dark corners."

"I can arrange for a couple of men to search the attic if you want," Wilson volunteered, his eyes glinting with excitement of possibly being so close to his quest.

"Thank you, but Mr. April and Henry are available to search for the chest."

"I'd appreciate you searching as soon as possible. Please, let me know the result."

"Yes, I will."

Wilson then broached the subject of whether plans had been made for our trip to Ecuador. He asked in such a way as to probe how forthright Barbara was being with him.

"Have you talked to anyone from Ecuador?"

Barbara turned to me. I gave her a half yes nod. She could handle Wilson. He already knew the answer from the tapped phone conversations between Barbara and Roberto.

"Yes," She answered truthfully. "I've spoken to a Roberto Sanchez about my intent to find my grandfather's remains. He is an Incan and has thorough knowledge of the Llanganates Mountains. I had him fly here so he could convince me to use him in my search, which he did.

"I'm asking Mr. April to go to Ecuador in the next few days to meet with Mr. Sanchez and prepare for our expedition."

There had actually been two phone conversations. The first when Roberto called declaring he had information about the lost expedition, and the second when arrangements were made for Roberto to fly to Boston for a face-to face meeting. The fact that Roberto's father, Paulo, the original expedition's guide, was still alive was never talked about over the phone.

"Well I see your plans are progressing. Please keep me up-to-date and let me know if you find your grandfather's chest and the map."

"Of course," said Barbara.

I could tell from Chuck's relaxed body language and his shift to small talk about Boston, and the weather, that he was satisfied with the information he had garnered.

"Well, it's best I get on the road. Tony, it was good to see you again."

"And you, Miss Anderson," he said, turning to Barbara. "If

the National Security Agency can be of further assistance, please call me."

"Thank you. We'll walk you to the door,"

We all shook hands, then walked to the front door where Gretchen was standing with Chuck's hat and coat. He shrugged into his coat and held his hat in his left hand. Then, he shook Barbara's hand again.

"Goodbye, Miss Anderson."

"Goodbye, Mr. Wilson."

We watched his car disappear into the moonlit night. Barbara turned to me, took my hand and led me to the library. For the first time, I sensed the warmth of the room which was softly lit by the fire. Barbara encircled my neck with her hands and drew me close.

"No more talk of business tonight, okay?"

"Okay."

Her full, soft lips pressed against mine, as she moved her hands to my waist. She rotated her hips to press against my hardness; it felt incredible. I brought my hands down to feel the full, firm curvature of her buttocks, and pulled her in tighter. With our passion swelling, she reached behind and did the unthinkable. She pulled my hands away, stepped back and took a deep breath.

"Gretchen has dinner ready. Let's have some wine, then enjoy a slow, full night of... dessert."

Chapter 15

It was after midnight and Barbara had fallen into a deep relaxed sleep with her smooth, firm mounded breast cupped in my hand. I snuggled against her and savored the fragrance of her ruffled hair touching my face. She stirred, so I rolled onto my back and soon fell into a deep sleep.

The morning sunlight filtering through both sides of the pulled shades woke me. I turned over to be against Barbara and discovered I was alone. There was a note on her pillow.

Dear Tony,

I had to attend an early morning school meeting and didn't want to wake you. Thought you would appreciate resting after last night. Gretchen will make your breakfast. I informed Henry that he is to help you look for the sea chest at your convenience. If you leave, please call me in late afternoon.

Barbara

After a shower and shave, I dressed and went down to the bright dining room with large windows overlooking the snow-covered apple orchard. A delicious smell of bacon, pancakes, and coffee wafted in from the kitchen. Gretchen had timed her breakfast preparations perfectly which told me she was very aware of what, when and where anything happened in the house.

As I sat down at the table, she came out of the kitchen with a pitcher of orange juice.

"Good morning, Mr. April."

"Good morning, Gretchen."

"Would you like some eggs with breakfast?"

"Two over easy would be nice. Thank you."

"Henry is in the kitchen and would like to see you after breakfast."

"If he's not busy, would you please ask him to join me now?"

Gretchen poured a glass of orange juice, put the pitcher on the table, retied her apron strings, and returned to the kitchen. A few moments later, Henry entered with a steaming cup of coffee.

"Good morning," he said and sat on the chair closest to me. He placed his coffee on the table in front of him and continued holding it with both hands.

"You talked to Miss Barbara this morning?" I asked.

"Yes, she wants me to help you look for her grandfather's sea chest in the attic."

"Have you ever gone to the attic?"

"Yes, I have, several times, to store things for Miss Barbara's parents."

"Did you ever see a chest?"

Gretchen backed through the kitchen door pushing it open with her butt, leaving her hands free to balance a carafe of water, two glasses, and pot of hot coffee on a tray. She set the silver oval on the table in front of me.

"Can't remember when I've ever been treated to such a mouth-watering home-cooked breakfast," I smiled at her.

Showing appreciation, she picked up the cloth napkin on the tray, flapped it open, and handed it to me with a slight smile of her own.

I began eating with small bites and turned my attention back to Henry.

"There are several chests in the attic," he said. "One does look rather like a sea chest. It's a deep, rectangular trunk made of solid dark wood with iron handles on each end. The others have a lot of brass decorations, leather straps and buckles. They appear to have been made to store clothing. The one that looks like a sea chest is by itself in the caged room."

"The caged room?"

"It's an area of the attic separated from the rest. One day Mrs. Francis had me store a floor lamp in the attic, and I asked her about the room. She said that her mother, Sarah, had the room constructed to store her husband's possessions. She believed he would return someday."

I finished breakfast. Gretchen cleared the table with a gratified smile when she observed there wasn't a bite of food left. Henry had just gone to fetch two flashlights and sweaters for us, explaining the attic had no lights or heat.

He led the way up narrow stairs from the kitchen to a second-floor hallway bordered with bedroom doors. A smaller door in line with the kitchen stairs opened onto a set of steep, wooden steps that ended at another door opening into the attic. Henry was right, it was a cold, dark cavernous space, and I felt that spirits were watching.

At each end of the attic, a faint glow of light outlined ventilation grates provided fresh air helping reduce some of the musty odor.

We turned on our flashlights and, safety-conscious me, stomped on the old roughly hewn wide pine wood floor to check its integrity.

"I did the same thing when I first came up here. The boards are solid," Henry said.

Sweeping my flashlight in a wide arc around the room, I noticed very little had been stored. There were several storage chests, two travel trunks, some cardboard boxes, a couple of standing lamps, an old rope bed, and an assortment of other things.

Henry led me to a small enclosure built with one solid side against the west wall. The other sides were enclosed with chicken wire. A door was latched to hold it closed, but wasn't made to be locked. We entered the area and our flashlights lit up an old heavy wooden sea chest with several objects placed on top. There was a pair of black leather boots topped in brown, an English saddle seemingly in good condition, and a brimmed cap with black velvet covering.

"This was Dr. George Anderson's fox hunting gear. He loved the sport and was a master of the hounds."

Henry continued to talk as he placed the gear on the floor, "Up until twenty years ago, we had sixteen fox hounds and four horses. Mrs. Frances, her husband, and Miss Barbara all chased the fox."

"Miss Barbara participated in fox hunts?"

"Yes, she did, and was an excellent rider and jumper. When Mr. George Anderson II was killed in Korea, the Fox Chase was abandoned."

Henry opened the lid of the unlocked chest. Inside was a discolored brown paper tube about three feet long, a dozen books, a black and red plaid wool shirt with a torn pocket, and a folded brown paper containing a small item.

I probed the tube with my finger and found what felt like flexible paper. Handing the tube to Henry, I picked up several books and read their titles. Among them was a book-sized black leather case containing drawing instruments: pencils, a ruler, ink, a pen, and extra pen points.

There were fifteen books in total. Some were histories of the Spanish Inquisition, Ecuador, and the Incas. Others were studies of Dendrology, Quinine, and Malaria. The remaining four books were the *King James Bible*, a Spanish English Dictionary, the novel *Ben Hur: A Tale of the Christ,* and a journal that looked to be about six by nine inches. Its cover was soft, brown leather with a sailing schooner embossed on the cover. Inside, it contained Dr. Anderson's writings.

I kept the dictionary, journal, and long tube out and put everything else back. We closed the chest and put Dr. Anderson's belongings back on top, arranged as we had found them.

"Thanks for your help, Henry."

"You know Mr. April, I'm thankful to have held some of Dr. Anderson's belongings. It makes me feel closer to him."

We left the attic and I went to the large library desk where I could unroll the map and weigh its corners down with books. It measured 3' 10" x 2' 9" but contained no geographical references of Latitude, Longitude, or distance. Notations were made in either Castilian Spanish or Quechua, but there was no indication of the map's origin, nor date published, anywhere.

I picked up the journal. Thirty-nine of its sixty-pages had entries. Hand-printed in capital letters at the top of the first page was CICHONA EXPEDITION ECUADOR.

The first entry was made on January 4, 1897:

Received $4,000 dollar grant from National Geographic to search for and bring back Cinchona bark and tree samplings from Ecuador.

My immediate interest was to locate entries referencing the map. When was it made? By whom? For what purpose? The doctor's next notes answered all those questions.

April 11, 1897

Met with Inca guide Paulo Sanchez in Quito. He is 20 years old. Started as an expedition porter at age 16 and is now a guide who has led three expeditions into the Llanganates. He knows the location of the Cinchona tree valley. Paulo stands almost six feet tall. His facial features portray his Inca heritage: High cheek bones, dark brown eyes, broad nose, black hair, and brown skin.

He wears a tan high-domed wide brim hat, heavy tan work jacket and pants that are typical of local workers. When he isn't guiding, he works on the family cattle farm located near the remote mountain village of Cota.

Paulo has experienced the unexplained loss of life on expeditions of those hunting the lost Inca treasure. He is possessed about Emperor Atahualpa's curse and will not guide me if I seek Inca lost treasure. I told him my goal was to bring back bark from different species of Cinchona trees, and saplings, and have no interest in Inca gold. He says he has heard that claim before, but after we talked, through dinner and the next day, he trusts I will keep my word, and has agreed to guide the expedition.

I gave him $500 in advance, and he gave me a copy of a 3' by 2' Spanish map that had a trail marked to the Cinchona tree valley.

April 12, 1897

Went to archives at Latacunga to do research. Sanchez's map was made in 1764 by a Don Atanasia Guzman which he copied from

Spanish adventurer Valverde's 1557 map indicating a written path to the Incan treasure.

The Inca people's belief in the cursed treasure started from the first treasure expedition when Valverde's derrotero was sent by King Charles V to authorities in Latacunga, who gave it to Father Longo as an aid in finding the treasure. On his quest, Father Longo vanished one night and was never found.

The next attempt was made in 1764 by Don Guzman who also vanished during the night and was never found.

The last entry concerning the map was made on May 5, 1897. Anderson was onboard the sailing clipper *Thomas* on his way back to Boston.

May 5,1897

Twenty-six days remain to reach Boston Harbor. I was curious about the details of Valverde's path that Guzman used to make the map. As I read a copy of Valverde's derrotero, I realized that Valverde had used knowledge of 16th century indigenous people to form the trail. The first sentence of his document directs: "Go in the direction of the farm Moya.". But, after 236 years, I doubt the farm still exists. Sanchez, thank goodness, doesn't need the map. He's been to the valley.

After reading Dr. Anderson's entries, it occurred to me that I was faced with several problems. Taking out my pocket notebook, I listed them:

12 March 1972

Tasks

- *How and when to notify Sydney and Wilson that I have the map?*
- *Start expedition to recover Dr Anderson's remains as soon as possible.*

Facts:
•*Without Paulo Sanchez, the map is not as valuable.*

Assumptions
•*Sydney will still find value in the map, somehow, and pay for it.*

The time of day had flown. By now, it was almost three o'clock. I wasn't hungry because around noon, Gretchen had brought me a ham and Swiss cheese sandwich on lightly toasted rye bread, some small whole sweet pickles, and a carafe of red wine, as well as coffee and water. She was some lady: Served a perfect lunch without disturbing my work.

I rolled up the map, put Dr. Anderson's journal in the top right-hand drawer of the desk and the notebook into my coat pocket. I also had decided to notify Sydney and Mike that I had found the map. First, however, I called Barbara on the tapped phone. She was at work.

"Barb, Tony. Have you time to talk?"

"Yes."

"Good, Gretchen has kept me well fed."

That was my way of letting Barbara know I was calling from her tapped phone, and why I was not saying anything about our night together.

"I called to let you know that Henry and I found your grandfather's sea chest and there was a map inside."

It was tempting to tell her about his riding gear placed on top of the chest but, then, I decided to keep conversation limited to only information I wanted to feed Wilson and Sydney.

"The map has notations in Spanish made to find the Inca gold, but it will also lead us to your grandfather's burial place."

"Are you going to send the map to Wilson?"

"I'll keep the original, and make two copies, one for Wilson and one for Sydney to buy. Right now, I'm leaving for the North End and will be home tonight, if you care to call. Tomorrow, you don't have school. We should sit down and make specific plans to get the expedition underway. I'm meeting with Bob Berry in the morning, then will come to Weston."

Planting the seeds over the tapped phone about Inca gold, Dr. Anderson's burial site, and our expedition plans was fruitless. How could I know they wouldn't sprout as expected?

Before leaving Weston, I found a printer on Tremont Street, downtown Boston, in the yellow pages. Then, I penned the initials, "TA", in the lower right corner of the map, drove to the Boston printer, and stayed in the small shop while two copies were made.

I sent one copy to Wilson for the Admiral Rickover committee. The other copy I kept for Sydney who would pay me for the map and pay dearly.

By the end of the day, however, Sydney never arrived. As anxious as he had been to get the map, I expected he would have called or shown up at my door. What I never expected was him never attempting to get the map from me. In fact, the next time we met was much later in the Llanganates Mountains. I found out why he never needed a copy of the map from me because he had a copy... with the TA initials in its lower right-hand corner.

Chapter 16

Barbara called at 7:30 p.m. with news. "Wilson called," she said. "I told him you found the sea chest in the attic with a map in it. He asked if you came across a diary. I said no. The only other items in the chest were clothes and botanist books. He gave me his home address and asked that the map be sent to him by UPS."

"I'll send it to him in the morning, I said."

She gave me his address and I wrote it down in my pocket notebook. We agreed to meet the next day in the early afternoon in Weston to review past developments and discuss future plans. I wanted Bob Berry to join the recovery effort, and recommended that, if available, he meet with us. She didn't object. After talking some small things, we said goodbye.

The following day, Bob was ready to go by one o'clock in early afternoon. On the way to pick him up, I stopped at UPS, and sent the map to Wilson. Then, I called Barbara and said we would arrive around 1:30. At 1:35 p.m., our tires crunched the hard-packed snow as we drove up her driveway to the front entrance. Bob got out of the car and waited for me to come around before going up the stairs. I rang the doorbell, and Gretchen answered.

"Good afternoon, Mr. April. Please step in."

We stomped snow off our shoes on the welcome mat and walked in. I introduced Bob and she took our hats and coats. Barbara came into the foyer, kissed me on the cheek, and took Bob's hand.

"Mr. Berry, Tony has told me of your good friendship, so I didn't feel the need to hide my affection for him."

"I also have affection for him, but I'll leave the kissing to you,".

Barbara smiled, "Shall we go to the library?"

The heavy brown-lined drapes were pulled closed. The only light in the room came from a low-wattage lamp on the oak desk, and the flicker of colored flames from the fireplace. We sat in comfort in tan leather high-backed chairs still set sideways to the fireplace.

Gretchen brought a pitcher of water, bucket of ice, and three glasses on a silver tray, and placed a notepad and pen on the coffee table. Bob sat on the opposite side of the table from us.

"I am anxious to get started." Barbara said, picking up the notebook. "I'll take notes."

"Let's review what has transpired up-to-date before we attempt to plan the expedition. I'll try to outline developments. Feel free to butt in if I miss something.

"The whole affair started in 1897, when *National Geographic* sponsored your grandfather's expedition to find Cinchona trees in the Ecuadorian Llanganti Mountains. A month ago, some seventy-five years after the incident, *National Geographic* chronicled his travels including the sinking of the ship, and the loss of the expedition.

"Admiral Rickover now has an ongoing investigation

into what caused the destruction of the Battleship Maine. He learned from the magazine article that your grandfather visited the Maine on the day it was destroyed. However, he was never called to testify about the suspicious activity of a fellow visitor. It has been established that a detailed account of Dr. Anderson's observations that fateful day were written in his diary.

"The diary was thought to be lost along with the expedition. The NSA (Wilson) doesn't want it found because Rickover's investigation may find the sinking of the ship and blame on Spain was actually a false flag. He learned about the diary from you, Barbara."

"Yes, he did. I sent Wilson my grandfather's letter to his wife in which he wrote about what happened that day on the *Maine* and that he had put the suspicious man's name in his diary. Now, attempting to get his hands on the diary, Wilson is monitoring our every move. Is he going to mess up our expedition?"

"No, he wants it to succeed for two reasons. One being, if the diary is found he'll make sure to be there so it will never see the light of day. Two the burial site is known to be near the hidden Inca treasure, and he also interested in finding it. He'll concentrate on the diary, and feed Sydney the location of the burial site to get to the gold."

"So, you believe Wilson and Sydney are cohorts?" Bob asked.

"Yes, Sydney has information that could only be known from his access to that phone," I said, pointing to the desk which held the tapped phone.

I, then, recalled putting Dr. Anderson's journal in the desk drawer, so, retrieved it and handed it to Barbara.

"Barbara, this is your grandfather's notebook. It was in the chest. I couldn't tell you over the phone."

She took it and with closed eyes, softly traced the embossed schooner on the cover with her fingers. Then turning to the first page, stared for a moment, and commented on his Remsen style penmanship, before putting the notebook on the coffee table.

"Have you read it?" She asked me.

"Not all of it. I was most interested in what he had to say about the map. I found his appraisal helpful in planning our expedition."

I picked up the notebook from the coffee table and read a few sentences he had written about the map:

My guide, Paulo Sanchez, gave me a map that he claims will lead to the valley of the Cinchona trees. I went to the archives in Latacunga and found its origin: In 1543 Spanish adventurer Valverde wrote about a path to the treasure on a map. His writing was still on the map when Don Guzman copied it in 1740, and which Sanchez then gave to me.

But the map is of no use to me. Valverde's guideposts were objects in nature and the landscape has undoubtedly changed after 455 years. The trail to the valley of the Cinchona trees can't be followed. Therefore, Sanchez is my only hope.

"Here's why he found the map useless," I said. "The only way the expedition could get to the valley was on the ground. They rode horses part way, then walked. They would have to know they were reaching a location described on the map by the end of each day. However, by 1740, most of the points referred to in 1543, no longer existed.

"Today, with the use of a helicopter, we can follow mountains and rivers described on the map to get to the vicinity of the valley, but we will still need Paulo and Roberto to guide us to the burial site. How far we must travel on foot through the jungle and mountains will depend on how close we can find a safe zone to land. The distance will impact how we outfit the expedition."

By now the fire had burnt down to tiny embers. Barb got up and put a two-foot split oak log on the orange glow that released an earthy smell. Bob and I used the break to drink an ice-filled glass of water. I poured a glass for Barb as she sat back down, then continued my talk.

"My hope is that we won't have to stay in the jungle overnight. However, if that becomes necessary, the health risks and cost of the expedition become exponential. Nighttime in the jungle is a total opposite environment than daytime. At night, insects swarm, and even with your entire body covered with DEET, diseased sand fleas, mosquitos, and chiggers bite. Snakes are always a threat. Nighttime stays require tents, sleeping bags, rain canopies, generator, lights. food, water, the list is long."

"You need a reconnaissance flight with Paulo and Roberto to find the nearest landing zone," Bob suggested, "they will know if it's going to need an overnighter."

"Well, we need to meet with Roberto ASAP, and ask him to be our guide. If agrees, he might get Paulo to join us," Barbara said.

"Yes, I agree. I'd already expected to be in Ecuador for at least five days to plan the search. To get the government to approve an expedition could take months and lots of money.

"A military coup just deposed President Jose Barra who was succeeded by General Guillermo. The General has taken an uncooperative stand with the U.S. over fishing rights off the coast of Ecuador. However, he does desire to improve the welfare of his people, and he hasn't prevented guided expeditions for North Americans yet. Roberto could possibly get a permit. But I know permission for a helicopter flight into the Llanganates will be nearly impossible because drug smugglers have helicoptered drugs into Ecuador from Columbia," I said. "He won't take the chance, but we can try."

"Barbara, by the time we rent a helicopter, pay salaries, travel expenses, and buy equipment, the cost of the expedition could be thousands of dollars. Do you still want to want to proceed?" I asked.

"Yes, I do. I'll get the NSA to pay for most of the cost. They want the diary to remain lost or the name of the man that dropped something in the coal bunker removed. Wilson knows from our calls to Roberto that we have a good chance of finding the diary which I'll agree to hand over sight unseen. They can tear out the page with the man's name on it, or whatever, on the condition the NSA pays for most of the cost of the expedition. Wilson will push the NSA to come up with funding because the expedition will get Sydney near the Incan treasure."

"Barbara, I like your style," Bob commented.

"Thanks."

"I believe we all agree that we need to meet with Roberto and get him on board before we continue," I said.

"Well, let's call him, and get a date to meet in Ecuador. He's in our time zone, so we can call today," Barbara said.

"You need a secure phone," Bob said. "We can go to my office at the station."

"Good. I haven't been to the North End for a long time. I'll have Gretchen pack an overnight bag."

"Barbara," Bob repeated, smiling, "I really like your style."

Later, I found our helicopter problem solved after reconnecting with my red-headed Special Forces drinking buddy. Who said drinking was all bad?

Chapter 17

We arrived at the North End police station around 5:30 p.m. It was already dark. Parking in the lighted police lot, we walked a short distance to granite stone steps leading to the front door. The night air was cold and dry. I looked up to see if the sky was clear and stars visible, a habit I had to judge imminent weather changes; but the glare from the parking lot lights blocked me seeing anything.

Through the door, we faced Sergeant Kelly at the night desk, well-known to Bob and me. He was a husky ruddy-faced Irishman who had been on the force for twenty-five years.

"Who be the young lass with you gentlemen?"

"This is Miss Barbara Anderson from Weston," Bob answered. "It was her chauffeur who was in the accident at South Tunnel a couple of nights ago."

Kelly leaned over his desk, taking Barbara's small hand in his large meaty one.

"Yes, I read the report. How is your chauffeur?"

"A few bruises, but doing fine. Thank you for asking,"

"You have two of the best to help you, Miss Anderson."

She thanked Sergeant Kelly again, as we walked toward Bob's desk area. The high ceiling fluorescent lights, and ten green-steel unoccupied desks, made the room look like a warehouse. Barbara sat at Bob's desk. Bob and I rolled chairs up so we could all hear the conversation over his speaker phone.

Barbara gave the international operator Roberto's number to dial. He answered.

"Roberto."

"Hello, Roberto, this is Barbara Anderson. How are you?"

In the background were strains of the song "Malaguena" being played on a Spanish guitar.

"Please, a moment while I turn off my music… I am in very good health. You have been good also?"

"Yes, everything is fine. I was so glad you came to Weston, and we were able to spend time together. How are your classes teaching English going?"

"The students are doing very well. As I mentioned, they are Incans who speak the Quechua language. Now, they are learning to speak, read and write English. I have them reading *National Geographic* articles about your grandfather's expedition into the Langanates, which connects to their lives in the mountains. They each have their own theories of what happened to the expedition."

"Well, I have decided to go into the mountains to recover my Grandfather's remains. Perhaps, there will be more information for your students soon."

"When do you plan to do this?"

Barbara raised her right hand with crossed fingers.

"I would like to come visit you to talk about how and when I should do it."

"It will be my pleasure to help you."

She uncrossed her fingers and popped up her thumb.

"I would like to bring Mr. April with me."

"Please bring him, however, I live in a one-bedroom apartment, so I will not be able to accommodate an overnight stay." His tone was apologetic.

"Not a problem. I plan to be in Ecuador for three days, but since I don't know how many days I will need, I can adjust my time. There are many things to discuss with you, but not now; it's best if not over the phone. Would it be possible on one of those days for you to take me to a remote Inca village?"

"Yes, I can arrange such a trip. Call me a couple of days before your time of arrival; I will meet you at the airport. There is one thing I would like to ask of you, Miss Anderson. Can you set aside an hour or so to talk to my class about your grandfather? Could you tell them about his study of the Cinchona tree as a cure for malaria?"

"Roberto, how wonderful to help stimulate your students' interest in science. I would be pleased to meet with your class. Two days before we arrive, I will call you. Thank you for your hospitality. Goodbye for now, Roberto."

"Goodbye, Miss Anderson."

Barbara clicked off the speaker phone.

"Well, you heard. We'll give Roberto two days' notice before we arrive."

"After we check our passports and required immunization shots are up-to-date, we can set the flight date," I said.

"Here's a suggestion before we pick the date," Barbara said. "Ski season is almost over, let's go to Mount Washington's hotel for a few days, and ski downhill and cross-country at Brenton Woods. Bob, I'd like you and Cindy to come as our guests," Barbara said.

"Thanks, Barbara, if our kids weren't in school, we'd go."

"Can you and Cindy, at least, join us for dinner at Anthony's Pier Four tonight?" I asked.

Bob called Cindy; she was delighted. With four kids, one on the way, and a limited budget, it was a rare night she was taken to an expensive restaurant. Thomas, their twelve-year-old, was a no cost babysitter, responsible and trustworthy.

At 7:00 p.m., we pulled into Bob's lighted driveway and Cindy came out the front door before Bob could get out of the car. She was wearing a vintage black military jacket coat, black fur bucket hat over her short, dark brown hair, and black fur cuffed boots. Her makeup was striking, and she walked with a confident stride.

"Are we in the right driveway?" Bob asked getting out of the car to meet her, As they met, he whispered something in her ear that made her smile and gently slap his face.

On the way to the restaurant, Barbara and Cindy shared talk about their lives after college. Cindy graduated from Boston College with a bachelor's degree in education, taught for three years, fell in love with Bob, married, had children, and quit teaching outside her home.

Barbara, on the other hand, never married, committed to the care of her mother. But she also had continued her education and became a teaching professor at Wellesley. It was surprising how close they bonded during a twenty-minute ride to Pier Four. Women have that special ability, I guess.

We were seated at Anthony's by a window overlooking Boston Harbor. This night, it was masked in black, no visible horizon, which made boat lights appear to move across a starless sky. As usual for a Monday night, only a few diners were spread throughout the spacious dining room. Every so often, the thunderclap of a woman's laugh would shatter the otherwise tranquil setting.

"Let's stretch out the evening," Barbara said looking over at Cindy.

We agreed not to rush dinner and ordered a white and a red bottle of Bordeaux. As we started a lighthearted conversation about being together in heaven, I raised my glass of red wine for a toast.

"May our companionship continue in the Hereafter."

Right then, our waiter brought appetizers: four stemmed bowls each having six jumbo shrimp anchored around their rims; the cocktail sauce resting inside the bowls decidedly giving off a pungent smell of horseradish.

The women had lobster casseroles for their main course. Bob and I each had three-pound lobsters. A family-size Caesar salad was shared at the table. Our waiter gestured and commented as he put each ingredient into the bowl. Starting with red wine vinegar, he added anchovies and garlic cloves, then two uncooked egg yolks, some hot mustard and stirred it all together. He filled the bowl with cut Romaine lettuce, then poured the dressing over everything. Lastly, he sprinkled in shredded cheese and placed croutons on top, then filled a salad bowl for each of us.

Bob peered down at his plate filled with a beautifully cooked orange-colored lobster complete with a boxing glove-sized crusher claw.

"You don't want to stand short in the land of plenty," I said.

"I won't, when you're buying."

Cindy, now on her third glass of wine, seemed carefree with a fixed smile. Her smile quickly faded when I let the cat out of the bag that Bob was going on the expedition.

"Bob what are you thinking? You have four kids, and I'm pregnant." With her smile gone, Cindy stiffened. "I worry every day you go to work that you might not be coming back. Now you want to go traipsing off into some jungle in Ecuador?" Tears started whelling up in her eyes.

"Tony, is it necessary to have Bob with us?" Barbara asked me.

"No," I said out of sympathy. I didn't want to say no, but I did.

"Bob, as of now, you're uninvited," Barbara said.

As a tear rolled down each of Cindy's cheeks, Bob looked into her eyes and held her trembling hand.

"Done. A win for the Gipper." We all laughed and went back to partying.

By 11:00 p.m. I pulled up to their house. They walked to their front door like Siamese twins joined at the waist. I was happy the evening had brought out intense feelings of love that are too often buried.

But I also realized I had just lost the protection of my wingman.

Chapter 18

At 6:45 a.m. I found Snow White asleep next to me. Barbara had stayed the night, lost inside a borrowed pair of pants and sweatshirt, under two blankets in my igloo apartment. I turned up the steam heat and by morning the "polar bears" were gone.

Looking at her face, I saw full lips slightly apart, and tousled hair that made her appear younger, and slightly rowdy. I laid on my side savoring her feminine beauty until 7:00 a.m. when I got up without waking her.

When she opened her eyes she said, "I didn't hear you get out of bed."

"You looked so content dreaming about me, I didn't want to wake you."

"I was content," she smiled, "dreaming about Clark Gable." I stuck my out lower lip disappointedly.

"You want a cup of coffee?"

She gave me a long kiss on the cheek.

"I'm going to shower first."

I put on the coffee while she showered. At 7:30 a.m., Barbara waddled into the kitchen in the sweat tent and, again, kissed my cheek.

We drank plain black coffee and ate Ritz crackers, the only edible available in my cupboards. After the gourmet breakfast, we decided to go for a walk before planning our trip to Ecuador.

I planned our walk to end with a stop at the abandoned fish processing plant. By the time we got there, our tee shirts were sticky. We took off our ski jackets, put them by the plant wall, and walked to the shaky wooden railing facing the distant harbor entrance some twenty feet above the wind rippled water which carried a strong smell of salt.

Aside from a red tugboat headed for Charlestown, the harbor surface was undisturbed. At the entrance, Graves Island, a 113-foot granite block lighthouse, flashed twice every 12 seconds.

"I can envision billowing white sails on the horizon pushing a Clipper ship towards Graves Light with the captain ordering a helmsman to 'steady his course' and 'keep the light house to port'. Imagine the joy of the crew returning after months at sea and probably having faced some perils to be safe back home."

"It sounds like you done some sailing," I said.

"Yes. I love to sail. And you?"

"No. I've never taken to the water."

"Tony, see those black broken poles sticking out of the water," she pointed outward. "They once supported piers where sailing ships loaded passengers and cargo. The schooner *Adventurer* might even have docked there when my grandfather walked aboard."

"What I see is the East India Company's sailing barque docked there, and the Sons of Liberty tossing tea into the water," I said.

"Are you a history buff?"

"I am. When I was ten years old, I read the history of the two hundred years of failure attempting to recover what was buried on Oak Island, Nova Scotia. Today, with millions of dollars available, along with use of modern construction equipment, the site designed to prevent discovery, still prevails. I… ahhh…"

Over Barbara's shoulder, I glimpsed a man disappearing around the back of the plant. "Barbara, go stand against the wall." She didn't hesitate when I pulled my Glock 45 from my ankle holster. Obviously, Sydney didn't need me anymore. He would get the treasure map from Wilson. So, Rocco would be free to put a bullet in me.

I sprinted to the plant's harbor side and sandwiched between a corner beam and the wall to listen. Someone approached but didn't attempt to mask their footsteps. Then a few feet away, I heard a faint tune being hummed. The footfalls went silent, but the humming continued. I peered around the corner to be sure it wasn't a set up.

A short, young tanned-man dressed in a multi-pocketed khaki jacket and black pants was there. He had put an open camera case on the deck and was fixated on threading a reload of 35mm film. Only twenty feet away, he never sensed me staring at him. I holstered my gun and backed away.

"What was that all about?" Barbara asked.

I gave her a short version of flattening Rocco's nose with my oak door, and how he slipped onto the pier a couple days later, spitefully shoving me into the water and declaring he would have put a bullet in me except Sydney wanted me alive.

"When I saw someone short like Rocco going behind the building just now, I wanted you out of the way in case he came out shooting."

We got back to my flat at 9:15 a.m., Barbara called Gretchen and informed her that we hadn't had breakfast and would like an early lunch. Awhile later, we drove up the slush-covered driveway to an area cleaned by the front door. Henry was outside, with a long-handled flat shovel pushing more slush off the driveway. When we parked, Henry opened Barbara's door, took her hand and assisted her out of my low-to-the-ground car.

Gretchen, appeared at the front door.

"Good morning, Miss Barbara. I can have brunch ready in twenty minutes after you want me to start cooking."

"That's fine Gretchen. We're going to be in the study. I'll let you know."

It was the first time I was in the library without a fire going. The open drapes revealed family photos on the wall by the doorway. I started to look at the photographs.

"Tony, let's make our reservations, and later I'll go over the pictures with you," Barbara was already seated at the desk with her hand resting on the phone.

"Wilson will know when we're going to Ecuador, if we book our flight on this phone," Barbara said.

"I'd want to tell him anyway. In fact, let's call him after we book our flight. It's Saturday and I want to talk to him at home."

American Airlines had the shortest flight time from Boston to Quito: eight hours and 53 minutes, with a stop in Miami. Arrival in Quito was scheduled for 6:45 p.m. We booked the flight for Thursday, the 23rd of March, leaving the return flight open. I wrote the flight info in my notebook and had Barbara dial Wilson. After several rings, he picked up. All I knew about his personal life was that he lived in Annapolis, Maryland, where I had mailed the map.

"Chuck, Tony April. I'm in Weston on the speaker phone

with Miss Anderson. Have you time to talk?"

"Yes. In fact, I was about to call you... bout the map."

"You got the map, didn't you?"

"Yes, it appears to be an authentic copy of the Guzman map, but it's been tampered."

"Why, what's wrong?"

"It locates the Cinchona tree valley where your grandfather is possibly buried, but there are blots making it impossible to determine the location of the Incan treasure."

"Well, the map was made to lay out a route to the lost treasure, yes," Barbara explained. "But this was not of interest to my grandfather. In fact, his Inca guide said he would not lead the expedition if my grandfather was seeking the gold. The guide believed, as does the one I am about to hire, that expeditions seeking the treasure are cursed. My grandfather's guide agreed to give him a copy of the treasure map only after making those blots," she said.

"Why do you care if the location of the Incan treasure is hidden," I asked. "Do you want Dr. Anderson's diary or the gold?"

"Is this really the Tony April I know whom I'm talking to? I have no doubt you have figured out the whole deal by now: Sydney is working with me to find the Inca gold which you know I've always been interested in since we were in Panama. But, first, I'm working with NSA to get the diary. Are you hiring a guide?" Wilson asked.

"Yes, an Incan named Roberto Sanchez that contacted me after reading the *National Geographic* article. He knows the area where Barbara's grandfather is buried."

I knew that Wilson already knew of Roberto from the tapped phone conversations.

"What I haven't understood," Wilson said, "is why you, or Mr. Sanchez, believe, after seventy-five years, there would be any remains left of your grandfather's diary?"

"Over the years, a few Incas have always known where and how the expedition was lost," Barbara said. "They know that my grandfather was buried in the ground with his belongings. I am sure that when we find the burial site, there will be some skeletal remains. The diary will also be intact since he kept it protected from weather in a heavy weather-proof brass case."

"So, why is Mr. Sanchez going to lead you there?"

"Because he's sympathetic to my need to recover my grandfather's remains. He's come to trust that I would never reveal information concerning the lost treasure."

"Are you prepared to keep your word, if you see an abundance of gold?"

"I will never betray Mr. Sanchez, the Inca people, or myself," Barbara said leaning her lips close to the speaker case.

I could see Barbara was planting reasons in Wilson's mind to push NSA into funding the expedition. She had emphasized the diary would most likely be found intact, and that she didn't want any part of the Incan gold.

"I've made arrangements to go to Ecuador with Mr. April next Thursday, the twenty-third, to meet and plan the expedition with Mr. Sanchez. I am sure it's going to be costly and have considered asking *National Geographic* to fund it in exchange for my permission to publish my grandfather's letter. You remember the one I sent you of his visit to the Battleship *Maine*.

In it, he describes observing a covert action of another visitor just before the ship exploded. This knowledge could prove that Spain was correct in asserting the sinking of the *Maine* was a false flag meant to blame it on them. Mr. Wilson, the visitor's name is written in my grandfather's diary. It can be recovered in the expedition to Ecuador. I plan to turn the diary over to *National Geographic* if they will fund the expedition.

"I have no doubt that *National Geographic* would fund you for that story," Wilson said. "Nor does NSA want to instigate an international crisis. So, when you get back from Ecuador, let me know what you plan to do, and the anticipated cost of the expedition."

"Yes, I will. Goodbye, Mr. Wilson."

"Goodbye, Miss Anderson."

"Nicely done," I praised her. "NSA doesn't want to open a Pandora's box, especially with Rickover's investigation interested in the origin of the explosion that killed 359 crew members and destroyed the Battleship *Maine*." I said. "You'd be a killer at chess."

Chapter 19

We arrived in Quito on schedule at 6:45 p.m. on the twenty-third. Roberto met us as we exited customs. His unfriendly manner surprised me and left me wondering why.

He greeted Barbara cordially, but when she began to introduce me, he turned away.

"Miss Anderson, before you check into the hotel, I insist we go to the Cafe La Casa," he said. "It is a ten-minute ride from here."

Roberto was quiet as he drove us to the cafe. Barbara and I looked at each other and remained silent. He stopped in a grassy parking area facing the café's steps which led to the front door of an old stone mansion. Roberto opened the rear passenger door, and we stepped out into the warm night air.

"Roberto, why are we here?" Barbara asked.

"We are here to determine if I will continue to assist you."

"Roberto, what's happened?" Barbara asked.

With eyes narrowed, Roberto looked at me and said, "Mr. April, I have received information, that if true, means I will not guide an expedition that includes you."

"What information, Roberto?" I asked.

"This evening I received a call from a man who convinced me that I should meet him before I met you at the airport. He said you sold him an old Spanish map and wanted me to verify its authenticity. I needed to see the map, so I met with him.

"As he was unfolding the map, he told me he'd bought the map from a Mr. April who assured him it led to the lost Treasure of the Inca and that he paid you twenty-thousand dollars, and a promise of five percent for any recovered treasure. He also said you recommended me to guide the expedition,"

Roberto's squinted eyes were fixed directly on me, "I didn't want to believe that you would betray Miss Anderson. He turned his gaze to her. "It is a copy of the map my father gave to your grandfather which marks the location of the Cinchona trees."

"What did he say about Miss Anderson?" I asked.

"That you manipulated her. Of course, says more about you than about her."

I could see Barbara puffed up and ready to blow some steam, so I cut in.

"Roberto, I know the fat man. Is he inside the cafe?"

"He should be. He was ordering supper as I was leaving for the airport."

"Is he alone?"

"Yes."

"Good, before he leaves, let's go have a drink with him. Roberto, listen closely to our conversation. After we leave, I will give you the background, and the reason he wants to stop our expedition. Roberto, believe me, I have no interest in the Treasure of the Inca."

The dining room had lighted candles on each white cloth-covered table. With dimmed wall lights, the atmosphere was very relaxed. Even in the low light and room filled with people, fat Sydney stood out dressed in a white three-piece suit. He sat in a far corner of the room with a napkin tucked under his chin eating a clawed lobster.

"Sydney," I said as we approached his table.

"Mr. April, Roberto, and Miss Anderson I presume. Please join me." He motioned with his fork to three chairs around the table.

I sat opposite Sydney so Roberto and Barbara would be closer to him.

We accepted Sydney's offer of a glass of Aguardiente red wine. He removed his napkin, moved his plate aside, and summoned the waiter to clear the table, bring wine and three more glasses.

He attempted to make conversation about our flight from Boston, but I waded in looking at Roberto.

"What did Sydney tell you of our agreement Roberto?"

Sydney smiled at me, acknowledging the start of our confrontation.

"I was told that you agreed to provide the treasure map for money and part of the treasure," Roberto said.

"Is that what you told Roberto?" I looked at Sydney.

"Yes."

"Did I get the map for you?"

"Yes."

"Have you shown it to Roberto?"

"Yes."

"Have you paid me for it?"

"No, but now that I have the map and you're here, I'll give you a check."

"Why didn't you pay me when I gave you the map?"

"If you had given me the map in person, instead of mailing it, I would have."

"The map you got in the mail was copy of the original. Do you know that?"

"I expected nothing less."

I asked Sydney to show me the map since he couldn't deny having it. He had already shown it to Roberto. He handed it to me, and I unfolded it and placed it in such a way that Roberto and Sydney could both see it up close.

"Look closely at the bottom right corner. Do you see the initials "TA" inscribed?"

"Yes," they both answered.

"I penned my initials on the map before I sent Chuck Wilson this map. Sydney, you never got this map from me. You got it from him."

"I don't know a Chuck Wilson," Sydney lied. "I got the map in the mail and assumed it was from you."

"Well, I would only hand over the map after you paid for it, which you didn't. I mailed..." The waiter arrived with wine and glasses, interrupting our conversation. With Sydney's approval, he poured us each a glass.

Sydney lifted his wine glass and offered a toast.

"Cheers, Mr. April, you've just saved me twenty thousand dollars."

Roberto joined me in acknowledging Sydney's toast with words I wanted to hear.

"I will guide Miss Anderson's expedition."

"Roberto, may you succeed in finding Dr. Anderson's remains," Sydney said raising his glass again.

"How did you know that Miss Anderson and I were coming

to Quito tonight?"

"Roberto said you were." Roberto's eyebrows lifted, a surprised look on his face.

At that moment, I knew something was wrong. Sydney wouldn't be so careless in his statements unless it was intentional. I asked more questions attempting to discover his motive, but didn't find out until weeks later. It had to do with a disagreement he and Wilson had.

"Did Rocco come with you," I asked.

"Yes, and before you ask, you can relax, Mr. April. He won't be sneaking up behind you again. He's already on his way to the treasure," Sydney lied.

"Oh, he told you about pushing me into the harbor?"

"Yes. I was upset because if you perished, I wouldn't get the map."

"So, he has a copy of the map and a guide I presume."

"Yes, and several men."

"I thought you wanted Roberto to be your guide?" Barbara asked.

"Yes, I did, but since I didn't get in touch with him until tonight, I had to get others."

"How did you get his name and phone number?" I asked.

"You must have given it to me."

I looked at Roberto, and knew no denial was needed. Roberto was back onboard and realized Sydney wasn't about to reveal his link to Wilson, or their intentions. I began to relax and switched to a more enjoyable conversation.

"Sydney, tell us about your travels and ancient antiques collection."

He talked in detail for over half an hour, and another bottle of wine. His talk was intriguing.

"We will be going into the Llanganates and have no interest in treasure so you can tell Rocco to go about his business," I finally said, wanting to prevent any potential confrontation that could endanger Barbara or Roberto. I knew, however, there would be no stopping Rocco from trying to kill me.

Chapter 20

Roberto took us to our hotel in downtown Quito. It was 10:30 p.m. when we arrived, all very tired. We agreed to meet for breakfast downstairs in the hotel at 8:00 a.m. After checking in, we all went directly to sleep.

That is, I tried to sleep, but laid awake part of the night trying to make sense of Sydney's game, and got nowhere. However, Sydney's possession of the map I sent to Wilson, confirmed their collaboration. Finally, I slept.

Awakened at 7:00 a.m., I showered, and met Roberto at 8:00 a.m. in the dining room. The morning sun slanted through the skylight of a small room onto dark oak tables and chairs. A businessman was reading a newspaper with his closed leather briefcase next to his chair as he waited for breakfast. At another table, a woman was trying to convince a child to eat scrambled eggs. The only other diner was Roberto seated at a shaded table with a cup black coffee. He stood up to greet me, and gesture for me to join him. Barbara arrived a few minutes later. The waiter came with coffee and menus. Our appetites spiked with the smell of bacon that drifted in when he passed through the kitchen door.

"I want to apologize for my mistrust of you, Mr. April. Sydney's possession of the map, and telling me you sold it to him, appeared credible."

"Roberto, I understand, and accept your apology. Let me brief you on what has been going on since you left Weston."

I summarized what transpired from the time of Barbara's first call to me through last night's meeting.

"I can see there are more complications than just recovering your grandfather."

"Are you still willing to lead the expedition?" Barbara asked.

"Yes."

"Thank you."

"What do you want to do while you're here?"

"The first thing I want to do is order breakfast. We didn't eat last night, and I am starved," Barbara said.

Without comment Roberto signaled the waiter who recommended the number two special: scrambled eggs, bacon, fresh rolled bread filled with jam, or cheese, a fruit dish in orange juice, and more coffee.

While breakfast was being prepared, I took out my pocket notebook.

"Roberto, I have listed tasks to do while here. I'd like to read them to you and get your input."

"I'll do the best I can."

"Ask Roberto to be our guide."

"I've agreed to be."

"Helicopter rental."

"What would you use the helicopter for?"

"We could pick up Paulo, and he could direct a flyover the burial location to find the nearest landing zone. Then, you could determine, from a distance, and ground conditions, the length of time needed to get to the site and back out."

"All that you propose would be helpful, except for you piloting a rented helicopter".

"Why, what's the problem?"

"I recommend you don't attempt it for several reasons: First, an American visiting professor wanted to rent an airplane for the year he was here. He couldn't fly an Ecuadorian registered aircraft with his FAA pilot certificate. The process to convert to an Ecuadorian private pilot license was so involved that he gave up.

Secondly, getting certified puts the expedition in jeopardy. The government, because of drug smugglers, requires detailed disclosure of flight plans. Once you alert them to the intention of recovering the Professor's remains, every department from Archaeology down will impose intolerable time delays, and money."

"So, what do you suggest?"

"What I suggest is hiring Bob Jones."

"Who is Bob Jones?" Barbara asked.

"Bob is an American adventurer married to an influential political Ecuadorian. He owns and pilots a bright red helicopter unrestricted in Ecuador. At one time, it is rumored, he worked for a drug cartel, but now operates within the law, and transports people and goods for a fee."

"Is Bob Jones about six feet tall, with red hair, and green eyes?" I asked.

"You know him?"

"Yes, we were in the same Special Forces unit. He helicoptered in supplies from Colombia to Ecuador. He always hid some hooch on board for us."

"What's your opinion of him?" Barbara asked.

"You couldn't find a better guy to work with. 'Rotor', that's what we called him. He was easy going, but if you wanted a fight, just make a school yard remark about his red hair and freckles.

Do you have his phone number, Roberto?" I asked.

"I can get it."

"I'll call him to make sure it's Rotor."

Roberto had a ten o'clock class and asked Barbara to speak to his students of her grandfather's work and expedition. Barbara was more than happy to talk with them. After breakfast, we walked the short distance to the University. Roberto got Bob's phone number, sat me at his cluttered desk on a swivel chair in his small windowless fluorescent lit office, and took Barbara to his class.

I dialed on the black rotor dial phone, "Alo, Jones here."

"You don't answer by 'Rotor' anymore?"

"Who is this?"

"April," I stretched out the sound of my name like he should know whose calling.

"Tony April! I haven't heard your drunken voice for years."

"You always thought I was drunk, when you were the drunken one."

"Possible. What's up?"

"I need you to fly four of us into the Llanganates on a recon mission to locate the area where a member of an expedition was buried seventy-five years ago."

"What's the interest in finding someone buried seventy-five years ago?"

"It's the desire of my client to recover her grandfather's remains."

"What are you, a lawyer, or an insurance agent?"

"Neither, I'm a private investigator."

"Well don't come snooping around my background."

"I've heard a tidbit about your doings after you left the service, Rotor. Someday, off the record, I would like to hear about your last five years."

"When do you want to go?"

"One of the next two days."

"I'm available both days. The local weather is good for both days. I would recommend tomorrow. Then, if we run into ground fog or rain in the mountains, we can try the next day."

"I'm calling from Professor Roberto Sanchez's office at Central University. He said he has met you."

"Yes, he has. I know him."

"He's one of the four on the flight, along with his father Paulo, myself, and a Miss Barbara Anderson. She'll pay for the trip."

"It's two hundred American an hour."

"She can handle it. I'll have Roberto call you with the flight plan and get your address."

"The helicopter is in my back yard, fueled, and ready to go. Adios."

I waited in the office for Barbara and Roberto. They came a little after 11:00 a.m. Barbara said the children were just delightful, well mannered, and eager to learn about her grandfather's research, and what she knew about his disappearance. They had recounted stories of the unforgiving dangerous Llangantes Mountains, and that anyone that sought the lost Treasure of the Incas either died or disappeared. Everyone believed in the curse but couldn't understand why her grandfather had disappeared since he wasn't looking for the treasure.

"Maybe someday they'll find out that it was about the treasure, but not of his doing," Roberto said.

I moved away from the desk so Roberto could get his phone and call Rotor. They arranged for us to meet at 9:00 a.m. the next morning at Rotor's house, located forty minutes from Quito.

Roberto picked us up at 7:30 a.m. the next morning. Traffic was light, and the ride was pleasant through the countryside. Off a packed graveled road, Rotor's 1000-foot uphill dirt driveway ended at a brownish-red stained one-story log home. A large barn, stained the same color, stood to the left with a bright red Bell 206B helicopter parked in front. No cars were visible.

When we pulled in, Rotor came out of the house. He was the same rugged tall guy I knew five years ago. His bright red hair had darkened as well as his freckled face, aging him. I introduced Barbara, the only one he hadn't met. He shook Roberto's hand and hugged Barbara. He still felt the pleasure of a woman's scent and soft body close to him. In New Orleans, he had been a big party boy, but I found out later that his life experiences drove him to a serious side.

He showed us a large topography chart spread out on the porch table. His wife, Maya. put a pitcher of orange juice, and glasses on the table before she left for work.

"Please help yourself."

We each poured a full glass as Rotor advised, "The weather is predicted to be good through late afternoon, so let's see where you want to go, and then, get in the air."

Roberto leaned over the chart. "First, we need to pick up Paulo Sanchez," pointing to his farm outside Cero. "He will then direct us into the Llangantes."

"Where in the Llanganates?" Rotor asked.

"From what he told me, it is in this area," Roberto put his forefinger on the chart.

"If you're correct, the mountain area you pointed to is a straight line one hundred miles from Cero which is forty miles from here. There are some mountains above twelve thousand feet which we will have to go around. The round trip will be about be 280 miles, and allow you twenty-five minutes over the area for photos.

The total flight time, I estimate will be three hours. At $200 dollars an hour, the bill will be $600 dollars. Is that a go?"

"That fine, let's go," Barbara said.

"Alright. Hop in the copter. Tony knows the routine and will buckle you in and get your headsets on."

I sat in the copilot seat, and Rotor fired up the copter. The altimeter indicated 9600 feet as we sat on the ground. The highest altitude indicated during the flight was 11400 feet.

We landed at Paulo's farm in 32 minutes. He was waiting, standing at the edge of a field normally occupied by cows. Roberto got out to bring him to the helicopter, and make sure he ducked under the rotor blades. I moved out of the copilot seat so Paulo could have a forward view to guide Rotor.

I was impressed by the agility of a ninety-two-year-old Paulo getting into the chopper. He appeared a lot younger than his years, having black braided hair, a dark brown face and hands slightly wrinkled. Dressed in black Levi jeans, slipped over black jungle boots, a tan snapped-button long sleeve shirt, and an old faded Boston Red Sox high crowned baseball team cap, most likely a gift from Professor Anderson.

Roberto introduced us. Paulo shook Rotor's hand and mine saying "Hello" in his perfect English. He greeted Barbara in Spanish, *"Bueno Dias Senora"*, to be respectful, as he held her hand. I put his head set on as Rotor rolled out the area chart.

"Paulo we are here; where do you want me to go?"

Paulo pointed to two small lakes joined together called "The Spectacles" in English.

"I need to start here. This is where we left the horses and walked."

"Ok, but I can't fly over mountains any higher than 12,000 feet."

Rotor lifted off the pasture and headed for the lakes.

"There are some mountains we will have to go around through the valleys. We will not get boxed in," Paulo said.

"Paulo, you are pretty savvy for someone that has never flown before."

"Yes, I was told about getting boxed in when I guided a group into such a place."

I could tell Paulo was enjoying flying and seeing places that took him days to walk now passing underneath us in minutes. Over the lakes, Paulo pointed to the North East of the Cerros Llanganati Mountains on the horizon, and asked Rotor to go to the farther one of the three, and keep the mountain on the left.

"As we pass the third mountain, you'll see a river in a deep ravine. Follow the river to the East to where it widens with a beach on the right side. If it is still there, the expedition camped 900 feet above it, and a mile upriver in the Cinchona tree valley. We walked to the beach most every day to clean ourselves and get water."

We followed the river that flowed through a forest of thick broad leaf trees and descended from 8200 feet to 1200 feet where we found the beach. We went past the beach area a few miles to where the thick forested high mountains ended and dropped down to hills, and then into the Amazon Basin.

Paulo asked Rotor to fly up the river above the tree line to look for evidence of the avalanche that buried the camp. A faint white defacement of the mountain, 400 feet wide, descended into trees below. Paulo, satisfied that he had pinpointed the camp location, asked Rotor if he could land on the beach so Roberto could walk across the river and check the forest undergrowth.

Rotor said he could. The large kapoc tree that had fallen from the riverbank near the beach didn't pose a problem. He landed, and gave us twenty minutes to look around. Barbara, Paulo, and Roberto got out. I stayed in the copter with Rotor to talk.

"I heard you were involved with a Columbian drug cartel."

"While stationed in Columbia, flying supplies to you guys in Ecuador, I fell deeply in love with Anita, a caring, gentle, beautiful brown-eyed Columbian woman. When I left the service four years ago, I intended to marry her, and met with her family. It turned out her father was the head of a drug cartel. He had three helicopters, and one day needed a pilot to take product to Ecuador.

You know how many times I've flown the mountains from Columbia to Ecuador, so I agreed to help. He paid me big money. So, for seven months, I continued runs into Ecuador until I made a fatal decision."

He stopped talking and I could see tears welling I his eyes. I didn't say anything. He took a deep breath, held it for a moment, and exhaled.

"Anita wanted to go with me on a delivery, and then on to Quito for the day. I liked the idea, and loaded a hundred ten thousand dollars of product, and Anita, and flew at sunrise to meet my contact, Carlos. I landed in the cleared jungle meeting place, got out of the helicopter and told Anita to stay put.

"Carlos should've been in the clearing waiting for me.

The chatter of the titi monkeys was more aggressive than usual which made me nervous. I sensed something was wrong. I slipped my forty-five into my waistband and started to turnback to board the copter and leave when two dirty, repugnant men, with Carlos's black leather silver buckled money case, came out of the brush a hundred feet away from me.

The dirt-smeared pint-sized one said in a heavy accent, 'You bring the heroin?'

"As soon as I said, 'Yes,' they pulled out guns, and started to shoot. Bullets whizzed over my head hitting the copter. I took the big guy down with a chest shot and knocked the little guy over with a shot that hit him in the shoulder.

"Then, I turned to check Anita. Tony, my heart stopped. She was slumped over; her head against the instrument panel. Blood flowed from the bullet hole in her forehead. She was dead. I tore my shirt off, soaked it with drinking water, and washed the blood from her face. Tony, she was beautiful even in death. Her brown eyes were wide open and seemed to ask if I was alright."

Rotor's tears flowed down his cheeks. For all the death we had seen in the military. I didn't believe he could cry.

"When I strapped Anita back into her seat and her head slumped forward, I went into shock, a fog, which lasted until the day of her funeral. After her family, friends, and I laid her to rest, I recalled what I had done in those memory-lost hours.

"As I was hugging her, I heard the little guy killer groan. I remember walking over and standing over him with the muzzle of my forty-five pressed against his forehead. But, I didn't pull the trigger. That would've been an easy way for him to die. Instead, I knew Anita's father would make him suffer, and have the pleasure of killing him."

"So, I took Anita, the little guy tied-up, Carlos's money case, and the drugs back to Columbia. After I landed at the poppy farm. I took Anita out of the copter and was carrying her in my arms, both of us covered with darkened red blood. Anita's father came running with two men, her mother not far behind. I looked into her father's wide eyes and said, 'Anita's been hurt.' Then, I collapsed.

"After the funeral, where she appeared peaceful, I told her father I could no longer stay. He understood, and gave me the helicopter, and the hundred-ten-thousand-dollar drug money. He thought of me as a son. I left for Ecuador. Ten days later, he got word to me that the little guy was dead. The product was then delivered to Carlo's boss, who said, that Carlos had been killed by the two robbers."

Rotor took tissue out of a box on the copter console, wiped his cheeks dry, and looked at his watch.

"Rotor, how is everything now?" I asked.

"Maya, a wonderful caring woman, has healed my pain. She is an attorney working with the Ecuadorian government, and I have never put her in a compromising position dealing with my illegal past."

"You see Barbara out there?" I said. "She's not just a client, she's also my love, and you have made me aware of how important it is to look after her on this expedition."

"Does this helicopter keep reminding you of Anita seated next to you?"

"It's not the same chopper. I traded that one the day I arrived in Ecuador, but I do, at times, see Anita in the copilot seat smiling at me."

"And you? What's been going on with you?" Rotor asked.

"I had told you about my sister being raped and murdered. So, when I left the service, I wanted to find her killer. I got my Private Investigator license, and with the help of Bob Berry, a Boston police detective, we did find her killer, a college professor. Like you, I wanted to kill him, but Bob stopped me.

Prison inmates killed him. I wish I had. The trial killed my mother, who wasn't healthy to begin with. But, seeing the photo evidence of her frightened little girl, nude, being forced to smile, that's what did it. I can't change the past. Now, Barbara has me living in the present."

During our conversation, Roberto, Paulo, and Barbara had walked across the river, through shallow, pebble-clear water to a muddy embankment. The crest was lined with tall thick grass and brilliant red, white, and yellow flowers with their perfumes being inspected by yellow black spotted butterflies.

The bank was steep, and a rope, tied to a tree, would be needed to help make the climb. Roberto crawled through the mud to the top to examine the density of the ground cover. He pushed through the tall grass into the edge of the forest. The near silence was broken by red long-tailed titi monkeys that hooted and pelted Roberto with tree flower blossoms. He ignored them, took a few steps into the ground cover, and returned to the top of the bank. He leaned back, dug his heals in, and walked down into the river, cleaning the mud off his boots.

"Twenty minutes is up," Rotor called. "Get back in."

Everyone came back and buckled in. Rotor lifted off the beach and headed back to Cero. Barbara reloaded her 35mm Konica, and continued her picture record of the trip.

When we all settled in, Roberto briefed Paulo.

"The ground cover under the trees is tall, dense, and thick-stemmed. Ten feet away from you, I would disappear. With the afternoon rains that come, it will take two four-hour days to machete a path the entire mile, you say it is to the grave from the beach.

Paulo nodded, "I agree. We need to come and work, then leave when the sun is out. We don't want to be in the jungle at night. That's when it comes alive with insects, snakes, and larger animals. Much more supplies and equipment would be needed."

Rotor advised that on a good weather day, the best time period to get our four hours in would be between 7:30 a.m. and 12:30 p.m. Hard rain starts in late afternoon that could ground him until dark, possibly stranding us overnight. We needed to return to the copter fast if we ever saw rain was coming.

Roberto said Paulo could read the signs of incoming weather, but each of us still had to carry an emergency knapsack with water, snacks, toilet paper, DEET insect repellent, a walkie-talkie, and snake antivenom.

"Roberto, can you make the emergency knapsacks?" Barbara asked.

Roberto said 'Yes' and asked Rotor, "What's the earliest time you could land at the beach?"

"With good clear weather, about 7:15 a.m."

"If all goes well, we can work five hours instead of four, opening up at least three quarters of a mile of trail the first day. Then, on the second day, work on the remaining quarter mile, locate the grave, and recover Dr. Anderson," Paulo said.

Before we dropped Paulo off, we agreed to open the window for the first day of the expedition in four days. That would allow time for Roberto to prepare the emergency kits. and for Barbara and I to buy the gear we needed which would all remain in Ecuador.

Roberto and Paulo had no restrictions. Rotor was available. The only unknown was the weather.

We dropped Paulo off at the farm and touched down in Rotor's yard at 12:42 p.m. He shut down the copter, and we were greeted by Maya as we exited. She was a very attractive woman with black hair down to her shoulders that framed a smooth light brown face, and dark brown eyes. She looked very tall and attractive being dressed in a white buttoned long sleeve sweater, black slacks, and open toe shoes.

Rotor exited the copter and suggested we go sit on the porch and have some drinks. As we walked to the house, he asked Maya:

"Anyone call to book the helicopter?"

"Only one call from America. He left his number and asked for you to call."

"Did he leave his name."

"Colonel Wilson."

Chapter 21

We sat at a wooden bench covered with a red tablecloth on
the porch. A vase of fragrant red and white roses in a vase
set in front of us offered a fragrant bouquet.

Maya had changed from work clothes into a white breezy
embroidered dress. Looking slim and elegant, she brought a tray
of *piña coladas* with pieces of pineapple, and a maraschino cherry
placed on the rim of each tall stem glass, and a basket full of
flaky cheese empanadas.

We sat in a pleasant warm breeze chatting, enjoying our
food and drink.

"These empanadas are delicious, Maya," Barbara said.

Rotor, who hadn't been talking, asked me why Wilson
would be calling him.

"I have no idea. Have you talked to him lately?"

"Like you, I haven't heard from him in five years. But I am
going to return his call."

Rotor excused himself and went into the house. Ten minutes
later he stood at the house door and motioned for me to join him.
We went to his office, richly furnished with a large oak desk

that faced a window with a view of his helicopter and barn. On his desk he had several framed pictures of Maya, a telephone, an appointment book, a note pad, and several pens and pencils in a cup. I sat in one of the two cushioned guest chairs to the right side of the desk. He picked up his note pad, sat down, and swiveled around to face me.

"Just finished talking to Wilson, and you have the potential to screw up my life."

"Don't say that. What happened?"

"He threatened me with a DEA investigation into my past work with the Columbian drug cartel if I didn't help him."

"What does he want?"

"Professor Anderson's diary."

"What's the problem? Barbara has already agreed to turn it over to him."

"He doesn't trust her. He wants the diary before she or anyone else reads it."

"That's bullshit. How does he plan to accomplish that?"

"He wants me to alert him when you are close to the burial site; then, I'm to fly someone in to take possession of the diary."

"Who is this someone?"

Rotor looked at his notepad, "A guy named Rocco. I'm to coordinate the operation with a guy named Sydney."

"Rocco, the half pint, and Sydney, the fat man."

"You know these guys?"

"Yes, I do. Rocco is Sydney's bodyguard, a thug that wants to kill me, because I flattened his nose. Sydney is an antique dealer obsessed with finding the lost Incan treasure. Up to now, Wilson has kept his association with Sydney a secret. How did Wilson find you?"

"He has someone tailing you, and they followed you here. He knew that you, Barbara, Roberto, and I lifted off at 9:32 a.m. and returned at 12:42 p.m. In those three hours, he established that I owned the helicopter, that I served in the military with him, and that I once worked for a Columbian drug cartel."

"He has the resources of the NSA. What did you tell him?"

"I was having a cocktail with you folks and would get back to him… to bust my balls," he said, "Yes, I know, on your porch."

"Rotor, I don't need to put you at risk. Tell him everything we did today with the exception of picking up Paulo. Even tell him how and when we plan to get to the grave site. There's nothing you will tell him that I can't handle. Yes, he wants the diary, but what he isn't saying is he wants the location that can lead to the lost treasure of the Incas."

We went back to the porch and joined the chattering group. Rotor and I looked to the road that fronted his house. If someone was spying on us, he was hidden by trees and shrubs. As much as we wanted, we didn't go look. We would play Wilson's game.

Four days later, we were all back in the helicopter, on a clear sunny day, skimming over the dense broad leaf trees nearing the beach landing zone. Preparations for entering the jungle were complete.

Roberto had fitted our emergency green backpacks. Barbara had added peanut butter and grape jelly sandwiches on an Ecuadorian sweet roll.

Rotor put the chopper down on the pebbled beach at 7:30 a.m. and shut it down. When we exited onto the beach, the noise of the helicopter still ringing in our ears, was replaced by the ensemble sounds of the morning jungle. The grey pebbled beach was wet with scattered pockets of water. Upstream, the river ran straight down the ravine for some miles to where it disappeared from view. A half mile downstream from the beach, it took a sharp left turn along lower banks and fallen trees.

Morning light was subdued with the sun still below the trees. The air temperature was 72 degrees with a steady breeze that picked up the smell of the river water. We put on snake gaiters over Levi pants tucked into snake proof boots. Paulo, Roberto, and I put a machete in leather sheaths attached to our belts, and Barbara hung her 35mm Konica around her neck.

We set our walkie talkies to channel 4 and put them into our packs. Finally, we sprayed each other with foul smelling DEET over our entire bodies, put on our backpacks, and were ready to move out.

The rain during the night made the riverbank muddy and slippery. Roberto managed to crawl to the top and stood in the five-foot tall grass surrounded by beautiful multicolored perfume-scented flowers and the fluttering bright yellow and black butterflies waiting for a rope to be tossed up.

I threw him the forty-foot white braided nylon rope knotted every three feet for a better grip. He secured it to a three-foot diameter kapoc tree and pitched the loose end down.

While he waited for us to rope up, he took out his walkie talkie, and called Rotor to ensure that they were on the same channel and could communicate in the event Rotor wanted us to get back quickly.

We moved out of the daylight into the twilight of the forest. Our unwelcoming party of titi monkeys hooted and pitched flowers at us that had a cluster of red fingers, each tipped with a small white blossom and a quinine smell. Barbara picked one up, and walked to the twenty-inch diameter, forty-foot tree.

"Tony, this tree is the reason my grandfather came here. It's a Cinchona tree. It would have been a sapling when he passed it on his way to and from the beach."

She was about to run her hand down the tree trunk.

"Barbara, don't touch the tree. Do you smell something?"

"Ammonia. Monkey piss?"

"Yes, the titis have marked this tree as theirs. Let's go."

Paulo and Roberto had started to machete a path up the mountain parallel to the riverbank. They worked together safely away from each other's slashing machetes.

I hung back trimming the trail. Barbara stayed further back still, picking up the large slashed pieces, and throwing them off trail.

She had grown accustomed to the bird, frog, and other small animal chatter and was looking at a scarlet Macaw talking to another Macaw hidden from view when she was startled by the sound of a freight train coming at her.

"What is that?"

"Howler monkeys."

"I never heard a noise so loud."

"No other animal on earth even gets close. They can be heard three miles away. These appear to be a mile or less. They won't bother us."

We stopped cutting the path at noon having made our three quarter of a mile goal. At that point we were about four hundred feet above the beach. We hadn't run into any snakes, and only once had to cut around a rotting log crawling with orb weaver ants.

I cut a fifty-foot path to the edge of the ravine cliff for a line of sight to call Rotor.

"Rotor. Tony, Over."

"Read you loud and clear. Over."

"We are on our way down. Be there in thirty minutes. Over and out."

"Copy. Out."

Chapter 22

Sydney called within an hour after Rotor set his copter down in his yard and feathered the blades.

"Mr. Green, this is Sydney Street. I understand Colonel Wilson told you I would be calling."

"Yes, he did."

"Were you asked to keep me informed about progress in recovering Dr. Anderson's diary."

"Yes."

"So, where exactly does it stand?"

"I believe they will get to the burial site on the next trip."

"As you know, Colonel Wilson wants my assistant, Rocco, to be there and take possession of the diary."

"I'm afraid that won't work. Rocco would be a fifth passenger and there isn't room."

"We observed you leaving with only three passengers: Tony, Roberto, and Miss Anderson. Where are you getting four?"

"I stopped in Cero and picked up a fourth passenger."

"Who is it?"

"A man named Paulo."

"What's his last name?"

"I don't know."

"Can you return and take Rocco?"

"Yes, I can, but it's going to cost four hundred dollars for the additional flight."

"In that case, maybe I will go along."

"Sorry, I wouldn't mind having you along, but if the weather turned bad, I could only make one trip out. I could stuff Rocco in the storage compartment. In that case, would you like to go instead of Rocco?"

"No. I'm not the size that can be stuffed."

"I'll call you when the flight is a go. Rocco needs to be at my house at 10:00 a.m. with the four hundred dollars."

"Call me at La Casa Hotel."

Three days later, the flight was a go, and Rotor notified Sydney. He put us on the beach at 7:45 a.m. and left to pick up Rocco.

We put on our gear and sprayed DEET on each other, set the channel on our walkie talkies, and roped up the slippery bank to the beginning of the cut trail. The clamor of titi monkeys greeted us, drowning out the rest of the jungle chorus. We adjusted our backpacks to secure comfortable positions. Paulo and Roberto had the additional weight of survival-style folding shovels. It had rained hard at night, and with each step, our boot soles sank deeper into layers of mud and water.

About a mile from the beach, through the cut trail, Paulo turned a sharp ninety degrees away from the ravine at a rotting five-foot log lying beside our path.

"I set that log to mark the direction of the expedition camp." Paulo said.

From the log, we macheted three hundred yards upslope to

a level area blocked by a ten-foot high wall of dense vegetation. With great effort and our machetes, we tunneled through the wall before walking from the dimness of the canopied jungle into a brilliant sunlit football-size field, covered with three-inch high, dark green dwarf monkey grass.

The field was bounded by a forest of dark, green-leaf tall Cinchona trees. We gazed at the field while breathing deeply, glad for the rest.

"This is the valley of Cinchona trees that your grandfather sought. Look above those smaller trees across the field. Can you see the pile of rocks left by the avalanche that came down the mountain?" Paulo said.

"Yes, we see it," I answered for everyone.

"The rocks, trees, and earth buried everyone except your grandfather. But the edge of the avalanche passed by him and felled a tree on him. When I found him over there at the edge of the field, he was dead. I took him from under the tree and made him a proper burial."

Paulo pointed to a large, irregularly-shaped dark boulder at the top of the field shadowed by tall Cinchona trees. "That is where your grandfather is buried."

Paulo walked us to the side of the stone that faced east, and pointed to where he had chiseled a six-inch wide, eight-inch tall cross. At the base of it were large stones placed on top of the grave, undisturbed.

"It is guarded," Roberto said.

I recognized the deep spiritual Incan beliefs both Roberto and Paulo possessed.

As we bowed our heads in respect, a large bird's shadow passed at our feet. Barbara momentarily stopped taking photographs and knelt in prayer. Admittedly not a believer, still I felt a spiritual presence.

"Your grandfather cared for the Inca people," Paulo said. "I cared for him."

Then, we began removing rocks covering the grave. Paulo and Roberto took the folding shovels off their backpacks and dug down four feet: at least a foot of it was wet sand, two feet of damp sand, and, finally, a foot of dry brown sand.

At that depth, they began to uncover brass buckles, pieces of leather strap, and patches of canvas. Paulo and Roberto made the hole wider so they could kneel and meticulously free articles covered in sand.

Barbara took photos of items recovered: a Waltham 1890 gold pocket watch, a Remington 1888 army pistol, two Blakemar briar smoking pipes, a Winchester folding knife, and at last, the diary enclosed in a 10 x 6-inch heavy brass case. The oxidation and tarnishing to all pieces showed only minor damage.

As Roberto handed each item to me, I sprayed them with oil, then wrapped them in cloth. As I treated the diary's brass casing, I was overcome by its potential to expose the secrets of the battleship *Maine*, it's fateful sinking, and the potential exoneration of a false flag which had led to war with Spain.

Incredibly, now, after three-quarters of a century of survival, NSA wanted these pages destroyed before anyone could read Dr. Anderson's notes of what he'd observed onboard the *Maine* the day it was sunk. I silently vowed to do all I could to ensure the Rickover Investigation would receive the diary before it was destroyed.

When I finished preserving each item, Paulo and Roberto began uncovering the skeletal remains.

"Paulo, Roberto, please stop," Barbara said.

"Is something wrong, Miss Anderson?" Roberto asked. Tears welled up in her eyes. "Grandfather would want to remain here with the Inca people, and the plants and trees he spent his life researching."

"God bless you," Paulo said looking up at Barbara, deep respect showing in his eyes.

"Roberto, please, just give me one of his ribs." She said.

At this, Paulo and Roberto hesitated and looked at each other. Was this a desecration?

"I'm going to cremate his rib. The ash amount will be small, but it is part of my grandfather. I will bury it with my grandmother Ashley, his wife."

Picking up the breastbone with a rib still attached, Roberto handed it to me. I broke the browned rib off, wrapped it, and put both the breastbone and rib into her knapsack as Barbara watched. When finished, I gently wiped her checks dry with my fingers. The solemn mood was disrupted by the noise of Rotor's helicopter approaching. He had returned with Rocco, the unwanted, to take charge of the diary.

Leaving them to reconstruct the grave, I went down to cut a path at the edge of the ravine for better reception to radio Rotor. After completing an opening in 40 minutes I called him.

"Rotor. Tony, over."

"How is it going up there? Over."

"We found the grave and the diary. Fill you in when we get down. Did you bring Rocco? Over."

"Yes, he should be up there by now. Over."

"Will call you when we start down. Out."

"Roger, out."

I heard Barbara, Paulo and Roberto coming down the

muddy slope. Turning to greet them, there was Rocco standing on the fallen marker log staring at me, holding a gun in his right hand which was hanging by his side. He had a Jungle Jim getup on: wide brim bucket hat, tan short sleeve breast pocketed shirt, high waist belted tan pants, and lowcut leather boots.

"April, you have a charmed life. Every time I have a chance to drop you, Sydney says 'no.'"

"Don't feel bad. You may get your chance one day."

When Barbara, Paulo, and Roberto got to the corner of the clearing, Rocco was no longer hidden by the jungle growth.

"You must be Rocco, I presume. You've come to take possession of the diary," Barbara said.

"That's right, lady."

"My name is Miss Anderson."

"I know. Where's the diary?"

To my surprise Barbara said, "It's in my knapsack, but you're not getting it. I'll give it to Wilson, but not you. I want a receipt that he has received it. I'll return it along with the expedition expense."

"That's fine with me," Rocco said, and put his gun into his belt. Then, he took the Guzman map out of his waistband and unfolded it.

"What I want to know is... where's the Inca gold buried, Roberto."

"I don't know."

"Sydney says you know."

"Well, I don't."

Rocco looked at Paulo, "I bet you know, old man."

Paulo remained silent.

"Well, do you know where?"

"You will bring the curse of Atahualpa upon us," Paulo said.

"The hell with the curse of your Inca king, you tell—"

Rocco's voice was muffled by the noise of a howling, heated wind racing down upon us. It passed overhead, blowing a wide hole in the tree canopy above Rocco. Sunlight and rainwater captured in many broad leaves cascaded down on him. The watershed washed away leaves and mud at his feet. Incredibly, a sunbeam shown down like a flashlight beacon reflecting off a ten-inch golden Inca sun disc, Rocco was nearly standing on.

"Well, look here," Rocco said, smiling broadly as he bent down.

"No, don't!" Paulo yelled.

Ignoring him, Rocco grasped the disc with his left hand. As he freed it from the mud, a black, brown and white-striped fer-de-lance shot out from under the log, opening its milky white mouth wide, unsheathing inch-and-a-half long fangs, striking him on the forearm.

Rocco jerked upright pulling all the five-foot snake's baseball bat-sized body out from under the log. He dropped the map but didn't, or couldn't, release the sun disc. He grasped the scaled whipping snake by its body, attempting to yank it off his arm, but the action only forced the curved fangs deeper into his arm.

The sun disc seemed to rise shoulder high, making Rocco's arm extended forward, dragging him toward the ravine. His boots made skid marks in the leaves and mud as he tried to resist being pulled. As he brushed by me, I could see the pale, yellow venom oozing from his arm. His eyes were opened wide, expressionless, like implanted glass. His mouth was gaped open in a silent scream.

Then, he made a faint unrecognizable sound. He no longer had control over his body and actually walked the last dozen steps over the cliff. The sun disc came off his hand and fell out of sight. His hat came off and floated behind him. Rocco, was falling now motionless and head-first, with the fer-de-lance still gripped, trailing him like a kite tail.

"Tony," Barbara said. "You could have stopped him."

"Probably."

"It wouldn't have mattered. He was going to die anyway," Roberto said.

"We were spared," Paulo said, relief hard to see on his weathered old face.

"I got a couple of shots. One, I hope, shows him going over the cliff which will prove you didn't kill him," Barbara said. Later on, I would be grateful for her quick thinking.

"I know you're still in shock, but we have to go back down. I'll call Rotor."

They all agreed, so I clicked my walkie-talkie.

"Rotor, Tony, over."

"Read you, over."

"Four of us are on our way down. Rocco won't be coming back with us. He fell into the ravine, over."

"Did you push him off? Over."

"No. Paulo will tell you who did. Over."

"Is he dead for sure? Over."

"Well, if his seven-hundred-foot swan dive into a foot of water didn't kill him, the venom of a five-foot fer-de-lance, that struck him, did. Out."

"He's dead. Out,"

Chapter 23

Rotor lifted off the beach and headed northwest to Cero, cutting off two legs of the triangle he had flown the first day to locate the beach. The flight direction blocked a view of the ravine and field where Dr. Anderson was buried. Still, everyone's eyes looked in that direction.

"I don't have enough fuel to fly over the ravine to look for Rocco."

"Just as well," I said.

Barbara, Paulo, and Roberto remained silent. I gazed down at the dark green broad tree leaves that carpeted the top of the jungle. Everyone was lost in thoughts.

When we landed in Paulo's empty, fenced-in cow pasture, Barbara smiled at him.

"Paulo, when I place Dr. Anderson's ashes in his wife's grave, I would like you and Roberto to be there. You are both welcome to bring someone with you and stay a few days. You can stay at my home or at a hotel in Boston, whichever you prefer. I will take care of all your expenses. It's my way of thanking you."

Paulo looked at Roberto and nodded.

"Yes, we will come," Roberto said.

Thirty-five minutes later, at 3:15 p.m., we were in Rotor's sunlit yard. We landed and disembarked before he tied down his bright red chopper. Barbara and Roberto went to the house and sat in oak rocking chairs in the shade of a partially sunny front porch. Maya wasn't home.

After watching Rotor secure the chopper, we joined them. Rotor went into the kitchen and returned with a pitcher of orange juice, a bowl of ice, and two long-stemmed glasses, placing them on a wooden table within reach. With only two glasses, it was obvious I wasn't getting any orange juice.

"Help yourselves, we're going to my office to call Sydney."

Rotor's hospitality was light years away from Maya's graciousness. On the way to his office, he detoured through the kitchen to the fridge, grabbing four bottles of Pilsner beer. Maybe he wasn't so bad after all.

In the dimness of his office, Rotor sat at his desk. I sat to the right side to be near the phone. We each popped the cap off a beer, drank, and discussed what Rotor planned to say to Sydney.

"Where do we go from here?" Rotor asked.

"What are you asking?"

"What do I tell Sydney about the way Rocco died?"

"Tell him you stayed on the beach and he needs to talk to me."

"Are you going to tell Sydney about Rocco finding the golden sun disc?"

"No, not now, but someday I might have to, especially if he wants Barbara's photos to prove I didn't push Rocco over the cliff. The photos will show him grasping the sun disc."

"What are you doing with the diary?"

"Let me ask Barbara."

I went to the porch. Barbara and Roberto stopped their conversation and looked up at me.

"Did you talk to Sydney?" Barbara asked.

"Not yet. Are you giving Sydney the diary to deliver to Wilson?"

"I'm not giving it to Sydney. I'll give it to Wilson when we get back home after he agrees, in writing, to return it within five days. He also needs to pay for our expedition expenses."

"Roberto, does the university have a microfilm processor?" I asked.

"Yes."

"What are you up to, Tony?" Barbara asked.

"I want to protect your agreement with Wilson that you have not read the diary. However, I believe from his illicit efforts to conceal your grandfather's observations, Wilson could remove or alter the pages, especially since NSA doesn't want Admiral Rickover's committee to have any information to prove that Spain didn't destroy the *Maine*."

"So, you want to document those entries," Barbara said.

"Yes."

"Okay, if you do, don't tell me. When I hand Wilson the diary, I want to keep my knowledge limited to only its removal from my grandfather's grave."

I looked over at Roberto and asked him to see me before he left, then returned to Rotor's office.

"Barbara is not turning the diary over to Sydney," I told him. "She'll give it to Wilson when we get back to the States."

"Is there anything else to know before I call?"

"No, let's get it over with."

Rotor swiveled his chair around, picked up the phone, and

called. It was answered on the second ring.

"Sydney? Rotor."

"Mr. Rotor, was the diary found?"

"Yes, it was."

"Rocco has custody of it?"

Rotor leaned forward, "No."

"Why not?"

Rotor sat up, put his hand over the mouthpiece. He spoke in a hushed voice.

"He wants to know why Rocco doesn't have the diary."

"He doesn't have it because he's dead," I whispered back. I heard Sydney's annoyed voice through the phone.

"Well, why doesn't he have the diary?"

"Because he's dead!" Rotor blurted out. Finesse is not one of his strong suits.

"What did you say?"

"I said, Rocco is dead."

"Dead! How did he die?"

"I wasn't there. Tony April was. I'll put him on the phone."

"Hello, Sydney? Tony April. Sorry, but Rocco is dead. He fell off a cliff into a ravine. I had nothing to do with his fall. He had the Guzman map out questioning Roberto about the location of the Inca gold when a fer-de-lance snake struck him on the arm. He became disoriented and walked off a cliff.

"Miss Anderson had been taking pictures; I believe she has one of Rocco falling. Would you want to see it? I also have the Guzman map Rocco dropped when he was struck by the snake."

"Mr. April, I am aware of the difficulty you had with Rocco, and I do believe your account of his death. To me, he was a close loyal companion. I don't want to see Miss Anderson's photo or need the Guzman map. You can give it to Colonel Wilson. I regret ever getting Rocco, and myself, involved in Wilson's subterfuge. I've had a foreboding of the alliance and was going to end it. Now, I'm afraid, it's too late." I finally understood that his purposeful but careless comments, at the Cafe La Casa dinner were actually made to break his bond with Wilson.

"Thank you for informing me about the manner of Rocco's death. But I warn you: Be careful, your life is expendable. Farewell, Mr. April." That was the last time any of us heard from Sydney.

"Now with Sydney gone, Wilson is going to call me," Rotor said. "What do I do now?"

"You have nothing to worry about. You've done everything Wilson asked of you. Just tell him a lot has happened, and he needs to talk to me to get all the details."

Rotor and I went back to the porch.

"Roberto I'll walk you to your car when you're ready to leave."

"I'm ready," he said.

Picking up my backpack, heavy with the diary in it, we walked down the driveway to his green Fiat sedan. At the car, and hidden from Barbara's view, I removed the diary case, and closely inspected it.

Dr. Anderson designed the brass case to preserve his writings. Though tarnished, the case was heavy, made of solid brass. A diary measuring 10"x8"x1" could easily fit inside it. The walls of the case didn't flex when I pushed on them, and had to be an eighth of an inch thick, or more. Two snap clasps were on the ten-inch side of the case which was sealed closed.

I handed the case to Roberto.

"You'll have to figure a way to open it. The case is in good shape, so, the diary should be also. I'd like the entry dates of

February 15, 1889, through February 21, 1889, copied. After you get it done, please replace the diary and reseal the case. Barbara and I are planning to leave for home in a couple of days. Can you get it done by then, and get the microfilm to me?"

"I'm going to the university now, and will have it done by tomorrow morning. I'll call you."

In less than an hour after Roberto left, the phone rang. Rotor went into the house, answered it, and came out to the porch.

"It's Roberto. He wants to talk to you, Tony. You can take it in my office."

As I walked to the office. I speculated why Roberto would be calling.

Maybe the diary isn't in as good a shape as I thought.

"Roberto, you have a problem with the diary?"

"I wish I did."

"What is it, then?"

"The case is empty."

Chapter 24

Nothing Roberto could have said would have shocked me more.

"What?" was the only strangled word I could manage to utter.

"The first thing I did when I discovered the diary was not in the case was to call Paulo," Roberto said. "He told me the avalanche knocked over a large tree which killed Dr. Anderson. Paulo said the doctor was lying face down entangled in branches when he reached him.

"To pull him out, he took off the doctor's knapsack, then removed Dr. Anderson's pocket watch, knife, and pistol before putting them in the knapsack. He said the locked diary case was already in there."

"Did Paulo have any idea why the diary wasn't still in the case?"

"He had one idea. While examining Cinchona trees, Dr. Anderson would often take the case out of his knapsack, remove the diary, then put the case back into the knapsack before writing his notes."

"So, he must not have put the diary back into its case before the avalanche struck."

"I guess not. Paulo said he didn't see the diary under the tree, and assumed it was in the case. Now, he believes it must have been pushed into the ground by the force of a tree limb."

"Roberto, I want you, Paulo, and me to be the only ones to know the diary isn't in the case."

"After all this attention given to finding the diary, aren't you going to tell Barbara that it's missing?"

"No, I want her to be surprised when she and Wilson open the empty case. Hopefully, her reaction will convince Wilson that Barbara doesn't know what happened to the diary."

"You'll be flying out tomorrow afternoon. I'll bring the case to the hotel later."

"Thanks."

I went back to the porch, saw beautiful black haired, brown eyed Maya was now home sitting with Barbara and Rotor. He was slumped in his chair, eyes at half-mast, trying very hard to be attentive to their conversation about Incan cooking.

"There's the Cafe del Inca in Quito which has genuine Inca food," Maya was saying.

"Would you like to go to dinner there tonight?" Barbara asked.

Maya looked at Rotor who had nodded off.

"The old man is too tired. I'll cook tonight. I don't mind. Why don't you stay here tonight? The guest room has a shower, and I've fresh clothes for both of you."

I nodded yes; Barbara said "Wonderful."

Rotor's chin lifted off his chest and with slow blinking eyes he asked: "Maya, did you say something about 'an old tired man'?"

"Go back to sleep, Man, the sheep are getting stacked against the fence."

He muttered something and fell asleep.

"Dinner will be ready in two hours. That'll give you both time to rest. I'll leave a change of clothes outside your door."

The guest room had a homelike feel and was furnished with a full-sized bed having a clear-stained, solid and curved wooden oak head board. Two oak night stands with alabaster lamps stood on either side.

A large oil painting of the snow-covered Sangay volcano in the moonlight hung above the headboard. A pleasant flower-scented breeze flowed through two screened, partially open windows. The bathroom, decorated with Maya's feminine touch, had a walk-in shower, single sink, john, and a mirrored medicine cabinet.

Barbara was in the shower when I heard Maya leave the clothes at our door. I brought in a silky black dress and some undergarments for Barbara. For me, she left a white Nike golf shirt, Adidas drawstring sport pants, and undershorts.

Barbara came out and tried on the panties and bra, the latter of which was a little too big. After I showered, I put on the undershorts, and we laid down to rest before dinner, happily cuddling, but too tired to do the nasty. At 6:00 p.m. we went down to the kitchen for dinner.

Lighted candles placed in the center of a rectangular table illuminated our dinner at a table that could seat eight. Rotor uncorked a bottle of Aguardiente merlot wine and poured four tall stemmed glasses half full. Maya placed a large red oval plate of thinly sliced grilled steak with a fried egg on top in the center of the table.

Barbara helped Maya bring in a large, red bowl of white rice and salad plates for individual avocado, tomatoes, and onion slices. The table was an array of plates full of colorful food and glasses of red wine, each emitting their own signature aromas.

Rotor started dinner with an attempt to repeat an old French toast that didn't go over very well with the women:

"Here's to thoroughbred horses, and women, and to the men who ride them."

"What kind of toast is that?" I asked seeing the women's unhappy expressions.

"You called me an 'old man' and you don't know the motion you feel riding a horse?"

"I didn't call you an 'old man', and you got your riders mixed up."

"Knock it off you guys, let's just say grace and eat dinner," Maya suggested.

The dinner conversation eventually turned spicy about some women aggressively releasing their pent-up desire for physical love with the advent of the birth control pill. I thought about Rotor's mixed up toast as Barbara rode me to sleep.

In the morning, we dressed in our own washed clothes and went to the porch for a coffee and pastry breakfast. A gentle breeze encased us in warm blossom-scented air. We were in a perfect, peaceful world until the phone rang. Rotor hoped it was Wilson looking for Sydney and the diary.

He wanted me around to talk to Wilson, but the call was for Maya. We were finally en-route to Boston when Wilson did call.

Before we left, Rotor had said, "When you talk to Wilson, make sure he understands that I've cooperated with him. I don't want him exposing my past."

"You'll be okay. Barbara is going to give him the diary."

On the far end of the porch, our expedition gear and Dr.

Anderson's rib were piled on a bench. The only thing we actually wanted to take was the rib. Barbara went to get it when Maya thought of something.

"Barbara, I suggest you leave the rib. You won't get it through customs. I'll get it cremated and mail the ashes to you.

"Thanks, I never thought about customs."

Rotor and Maya dropped us off at the hotel by 8:30 a.m. Barbara invited them to Weston some day and to vacation in New England with us. Maya was excited, Rotor wasn't. He whispered to me while Maya was helping Barbara pack, "I would love to get back in the States, but Wilson could get me arrested."

After warm hugs and broad smiles, they left, and we waited for our flight.

By 9:00 a.m. Roberto brought the diary case. We sat and talked for half an hour before he said goodbye. At 3:30 p.m. we flew American Airlines home, arriving in Boston at 6:20 p.m.

Henry met us in the Customs lobby and suggested we put on jackets. The short walk to the waiting Bentley was in dark and damp, windy and frigid winter air. It was quite a jolt.

"Henry, I noticed you have on new chauffeur attire," Barbara said.

"Yes, Ma'am. I never got the blood stain off my old set. The Bentley we're riding in is yours, however, repaired and good as new."

"I'll be going to the North End in the morning. How's my car?" I asked.

"Ready to go. I have it in a horse stall and have been running it every couple of days."

Henry dropped us off at the front door and brought in our luggage. Gretchen, in her black dress came out of the kitchen wiping her hands on her apron and reached out to take our coats while welcoming us home.

"I have some hot chicken soup with noodles and chicken chunks, if you're hungry."

"Yes, I'm starved," Barbara said.

"Mr. April, a Mr. Rotor called. He wants you to call him as soon as you get in. I put his number on the library desk."

"Thanks, I'll call him after we eat." After having Gretchen's soup, I went to the library and called Rotor on the tapped phone.

"Rotor? Tony. What's up?"

"Wilson called looking for Sydney. He was irritated that he hadn't heard from him. Said he called Sydney's hotel and was told he had checked out two days ago. Wilson wanted to know if I had seen or, at least, talked to him. I told him you had talked with him yesterday afternoon. Then, our conversation went like this: He asked me:

'Does he have the diary?'

'No.'

'You mean, they didn't find it?'

'Yes, they found it.'

'Well, where is it?'

'Miss Anderson has the diary and plans to give it to you when she gets home.'

'Why doesn't Sydney have it?'

'It's a long story. You have to talk to April.'

'When are they getting back?'

'They should be back tonight.'

'If you talk to him before I do, tell him I'm flying in tomorrow to pick up the diary."

"That was all, then we hung up. I just thought you

should know."

"Thanks for the info, Rotor."

Knowing Barbara's phone was still tapped, I could have calculated the next call. It came ten minutes after I got off the phone with Rotor. I knew that Wilson knew Barbara had the diary.

"Tony, I'm flying into Logan tomorrow to pick up the diary. Can you and Miss Anderson meet me at the Statler Hotel at 3:00 p.m.?"

"Hold on while I get Miss Anderson on the phone." I beckoned for Barbara to take the phone.

"Colonel Wilson, this is Miss Anderson. Yes, we can meet with you, provided you bring a letter stating that NSA will return the diary within five days, and you also need to bring twenty thousand dollars for the cost of the expedition."

"I will bring the letter and the money."

"Perfect. Then, we will be at the Statler tomorrow at 3:00 p.m."

After Barbara hung up, I called detective Bob Berry, and we agreed to have lunch at 1:00 p.m. at Peter's Restaurant. In the morning, I drove my car to the North End. Henry would take Barbara to the Statler; I would join her later.

At my apartment, I turned up the thermostat from 55 to 68, tossed the curdled milk and all the food later than it's "eat by" date. No one was home upstairs, so I couldn't get my saved mail.

Removing my topcoat and hat, I put a sweater on, grabbed a beer, and sat in the warm sunlight coming through the den window. I pushed my stuffed recliner back a little less than vertical, nursed a beer, and pondered why exposing the sinking of *Maine* as a false flag mattered so much to me.

I thought about all my classmates who were slaughtered in the needless false flag war of Vietnam. How McNamara, the Secretary of Defense, withheld from President Johnson the information that North Vietnam patrol boats had never attacked our destroyers, which then resulted in the President declaring war.

I thought about the Pentagon's Operation Northwoods proposal to commit a series of false flags which included blowing up a U.S. ship in Guantanamo Bay and putting the blame on Cuba. The proposal verified the willingness of hawks to kill their own to go to war. Fortunately. President Kennedy vetoed the proposal.

I mused, if the *Maine* sinking was proven to be a false flag, maybe the war cry, "Remember the *Maine*" would turn to be a rallying call to Congress to take back its Constitutional grant of being the sole power to declare war.

Now with Dr. Anderson's diary being lost, Admiral Rickover's investigation wouldn't have the evidence to conclude the real facts about a false flag. NSA would be off the hook.

My mulling ended when I noticed the beer bottle was empty, and it was past noon. Twenty minutes later, I walked out of the cold into Pete's warm restaurant. Bob was sitting at our usual table next to the window where a passerby could look in and see what we were eating. It had been nearly two months since I last saw him.

"How's Peggy and the kids?" I asked.

"They're all fine. But they miss their Uncle Tony."

"Tell them I coming to see them as soon as I get settled. What's up with you?"

"Still working the Gibbs homicide. No leads. The case is getting cold. You never called me from Ecuador," Bob said.

"I Know. I should've called to fill you in on what was going on. I got so wound up caring for Barbara and planning the expedition that I didn't remember to call. The only threat turned out to be Rocco, and he was killed when he fell off a cliff."

"So, you finally killed the little bastard."

"No, but I could have stopped him from going over the edge."

"What happened?"

Instead of isolating Rocco's story, I summarized the entire expedition and players: Roberto, Paulo, Rotor, Wilson, Sydney, Rocco, Barbara, and myself.

I was voicing my frustration about the lost diary when Peter brought lunch with its aromatic blend of spicy sausage, peppers, onions, fresh baked Italian bread, and glasses of Chianti wine.

"I have not seen you for a long time. No racquetball?" Peter asked me.

"Tony has been in Ecuador looking for a body." Bob said.

"Yes, they have lots of good women there," Peter said.

"He was looking for a dead one."

Peter bowed and left. After Bob devoured his food, he gave me his take on the sinking of the ship.

"I agree that the *Maine* could have been intentionally sunk. The Hearst and Pulitzer newspapers then were pounding the public with exaggerated stories of Cuban people suffering at the hands of Spain. Every day articles pushed for the liberation of Cuba. So, a significant event was needed to go to war. Sinking the *Maine* in Havana Harbor would certainly have done it." Bob said.

"Exactly. The Navy Board of Inquiry blamed it on a Spanish mine, totally rejecting other potential causes. They also denied Dr. Anderson a hearing that would have revealed the name and description of the person he saw drop a small tube into the coal bunker. Now, that person will never be known. NSA will be happy to learn the diary is lost, but I'm not."

"You may as well relax. The Rickover Investigation might come up with something."

"Right now, I can't relax. In forty-five minutes, I have to deal with both Barbara and Wilson when they discover the diary case is empty."

Chapter 25

I met Barbara in the hotel lobby at 2:45 p.m. Together, we went up to room 224. When Wilson answered the door, I was surprised to see another man getting up from a desk chair to also greet us. He was young, maybe late twenties, short, dark skinned, black eyes and hair, with a bright white toothy smile.

"I am Tommy Sing," he introduced himself. "Mr. Wilson has told me about your adventure to Ecuador. I am most anxious to read your grandfather's diary, Miss Anderson.

"Tommy is an analyst with the agency," Wilson said. "Before we pay you for the expedition, he needs to authenticate that it's your grandfather's diary. He will then remove any classified material. After that, you can take the diary with you."

I looked at the desk where Tommy had draped his coat over its chair and saw a bottle of black ink and fountain pen ready to redact the diary. That would immediately wipe out the name of the man who could have caused the false flag. It would be gone forever. Then, I mused that Tommy wouldn't need his ink because the diary wasn't in its case.

"Can I get you folks a drink?" Wilson asked.

Barbara said she would like some water. He retrieved a bottle out of the room's small refrigerator. As he walked, I noticed his $900 John Lobb black shoes, and the smell of Pierre Cardin cologne. Chuck Wilson hadn't lost his extravagant taste.

"Miss Anderson, I talked to Rotor and he said you have the diary."

"Yes, I have it in my purse."

"Why didn't you give it to Sydney?"

"Sydney didn't want the diary," I butted in. "He said he wouldn't work with you any longer."

"Really? What brought that on?"

"Probably his death. Rocco found an Incan gold sun disc while waiting to take possession of the diary. As he picked up the disc, he was pulled off a nearby cliff."

"Who pulled him off?"

"Paulo, the man who led us to where he buried Dr. Anderson, said it was the spirit of Atahualpa."

Barbara stared at me. At the end of the day, she would also learn why I revealed that Paulo was her grandfather's expedition guide, and about the existence of the gold sun disc.

"I knew Paulo was with you, but didn't know he was Dr. Anderson's expedition guide."

"Sydney was devastated over Rocco's death and blames himself for getting Rocco involved with you. So, he's done with hunting for Inca treasure, and helping you with the diary."

"He should blame Atahualpa's bullshit curse."

"I have the Guzman map that Rocco dropped, but if you're going to go after the treasure, you won't need it. All you'll need do is walk the path we cut through the jungle to where it turns a sharp ninety degrees. That's where Rocco found the sun disc."

Tommy looked uncomfortable hearing the conversation but said nothing.

"We'll talk about that later. Please give me the diary, Miss Anderson."

Here we go, I mused.

Barbara handed the heavy brass case to Wilson, confident the diary was inside. Wilson placed the tarnished case on the coffee table and, with his thumb, flipped open the locking snaps. Barbara leaned forward as he opened the case. Then shock. Everyone could see it was empty.

Barbara jerked up, "Tony! The diary isn't in the case!"

"I see that," I said.

Wilson was studying our reactions. He seemed convinced by Barbara's body language that she didn't remove the diary. But he wasn't sure about me.

"Where's the diary, Tony?"

"Where's the diary? Unfortunately, since it's not in the case, it doesn't exist,"

"What?" Barbara asked.

I looked at Wilson and Tommy.

"Our agreement, which we have kept, was not to open the diary case. The day before we left Ecuador I started to fret about the diary. I called Paulo. 'Paulo is there any possibility that the diary isn't in the case?'

"'Yes.' He told me, 'When the avalanche came, I wasn't in the area, so I couldn't see if Dr. Anderson had the diary out making notes about trees, which he usually did. When I pulled his body out from under the tree that killed him, I found his eyeglasses near him, but didn't see the diary. I looked in his knapsack. The locked diary case was there, and I assumed the diary was in it.'"

"So, gentlemen, now we know the diary isn't in the case. Miss Andersen doesn't have it. I don't have it. Obviously, Chuck, you don't have it. The only reasonable conclusion is that it remained on the mountain and has not survived insects and weather over the past seventy years. Therefore, it doesn't exist," I concluded.

"If I could believe you don't have the diary, Tony, then I would agree it's been destroyed," Wilson said.

"Chuck, if I ever had the diary, I would have given it to Rickover, and you would know it. There is nothing more I would like to see proven than the sinking of the *Maine* was a false flag."

"Tony, you're getting carried away now."

"Really? You've tapped Miss Anderson's phone, drove her chauffeur into an abutment, scraped evidence off her damaged Bentley, threatened Ro—."

Chuck interrupted, "That's enough!"

Tommy said nothing. He put the ink bottle, ink pen, and expedition check back into his brief case and stood, expressionless, looking at Wilson.

"Are we done here?" Barbara asked.

"I'll take the tap off your phone, Miss Anderson," Chuck said as he escorted us to the elevator.

Barbara put her sunglasses on as we walked out of the hotel.

"Tony, you knew the diary wasn't in the case the entire time, and you didn't tell me."

"Barbara, I hoped your true reaction on seeing the empty case, would convince Wilson you didn't have the diary. It did."

"I told him about Paulo to prove the diary was left on the mountain. As far as Rocco finding the sun disc, Wilson doesn't believe in curses. He'll go after the treasure. He won't bother you anymore."

"I hoped to have my grandfather's diary."

"At least you have his rib... or will have soon." I stopped walking in the middle of the parking lot and took off her sunglasses. Looking into her questioning emerald eyes, the words came out so easily:

"Will you marry me?"

"Yes, I will."

Two months later Rotor wasn't worried about coming to Weston. After Wilson had learned about everything that happened on the expedition, he bargained with Rotor to helicopter him to the location where Rocco found the Incan sun disc in exchange for cleaning Rotor's drug cartel record. The bargain was kept.

On September 1, 1974, we were married. Bob Berry was my best man. Maya and Rotor came from Ecuador and brought Dr. Anderson's ashes in a solid brass urn. Barbara kept the urn on the study's fireplace mantel until the ashes were buried with her mother, on October 6, 1975, with Paulo and Roberto present.

By that date Barbara was pregnant, the phone tap had been removed, and the Rickover Investigation was still ongoing without Dr. Anderson's diary.

When Bob called January 6, 1976, the sinking of the *Maine* had faded from my mind. All my energy and attention was directed to being a thoughtful loving husband, and father to our precious healthy four-month old black-haired, blue-eyed, Marie. Our second child, the little boy I wanted, George Anderson, was born a year later.

"Tony, I just received an advance copy of Rickover's report,

'How the Battleship *Maine* was Destroyed,'" Bob Berry said. "His investigator concluded the destruction wasn't caused by a Spanish mine, but initiated by an internal explosion of the coal bunker."

The conclusion that the coal bunker explosion set off the magazine stores was not well received by hawks who promote the cause as being a Spanish mine. Never mind there was no evidence to the contrary of no fish being killed as a mine would have done, nor water geyser being observed by crew survivors. They also couldn't explain the sound of two explosions that were heard that day on board the ship.

"Did he say why the coal bunker exploded?"

"A spontaneous combustion of the coal," Bob said.

"Well, that had to be the most convenient spontaneous combustion for the hawks and press who needed a significant event to go to war with Spain. For the Battleship *Maine* to be destroyed in Havana Harbor by a spontaneous combustion in the coal bunker and have it happen just when it was needed is improbable," I said.

"However, either way, whether someone dropped a timed incendiary device into the coal bunker, or the evidence of a mine being present was intentionally distorted to go to war with Spain, the destruction of the Battleship *Maine* was a false flag."

Acknowledgments

Thanks to everyone who made *False Flag* possible, especially Andrea Watson for her assistance in formatting the manuscript and proof reading.

About the Author

A native of Lawrence, MA, Jay Barrett attended the US Naval Academy as well as Tri-State College where he received a degree in Mechanical Engineering. He worked for General Dynamics as a flight test engineer on intercept and guidance systems for fighter jets in the US and Europe. Subsequent to this he worked at AVCO as a project engineer in the development of ballistic missiles prior to transitioning to the investment world. Jay also worked as a character model for an advertising agency, playing everything from a criminal to a priest. Ultimately he worked as a golf instructor to the corporate world.

Jay's interests and accomplishments are many and include becoming a championship squash player in the US and Europe. His love of the sea led him SCUBA diving, searching for shipwrecks in New England and the Great Lakes.

The father of five, Jay now lives in Central Florida. *False Flag* is his first book, with a second one close to completion.

Made in the USA
Middletown, DE
27 June 2020